"Why don't you ask one of your girlfriends to be your fiancée?" Flora asked Matt unevenly

"I couldn't make this kind of deal with any of the girls I know."

"I don't see why not," said Flora.

"They might take me seriously, for a start...."

"Whereas my feelings don't matter! I'm just your assistant—is that what you mean?"

"No, it's not what I mean. But you won't get emotionally involved. You've made it clear that your priority is to travel and, anyway, wasn't it you who said that we were made for each other?"

We were made for each other, darling. Flora's words on the plane when they had first met seemed to reverberate now in the air between them....

From boardroom...to bride and groom!

Dear Reader,

Welcome to the third book in our MARRYING THE BOSS miniseries.

Over the following months, some of your favorite Harlequin Romance® authors will be bringing you a variety of tantalizing stories about love in the workplace!

Falling for the boss can mean trouble, so our gorgeous heroes and lively heroines all struggle to resist their feelings of attraction for each other. But somehow love always ends up top of the agenda. And it isn't just a nine-to-five affair.... Mixing business with pleasure carries on after hours—and ends in marriage!

Happy reading!

The Editors

Look out next month for the fourth in our
MARRYING THE BOSS series:
Beauty and the Boss by Lucy Gordon
Harlequin Romance #3548

Temporary Engagement
Jessica Hart

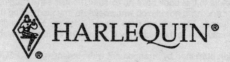

HARLEQUIN®

TORONTO • NEW YORK • LONDON
AMSTERDAM • PARIS • SYDNEY • HAMBURG
STOCKHOLM • ATHENS • TOKYO • MILAN • MADRID
PRAGUE • WARSAW • BUDAPEST • AUCKLAND

ISBN 0-373-03544-6

TEMPORARY ENGAGEMENT

First North American Publication 1999.

Printed in U.S.A.

CHAPTER ONE

'HERE he is now.' The pilot nodded across the tarmac to where a sleek black car had just appeared from the direction of the terminal. He straightened from where he had been leaning against the steps while he chatted to Flora. 'I'd better get going. Matt Davenport doesn't like to be kept waiting.' He winked at her. 'Good luck!'

'Thanks,' said Flora in a hollow voice as he took the steps up to the plane two at a time. She watched the car approach with a sinking heart. If anyone else wished her luck in dealing with Matt Davenport, she would start to get really nervous!

An unseasonably cold wind for late May blew her hair across her face, and she shook her head to keep it out of her eyes as she danced from foot to foot, hugging her bag to her chest to keep herself warm. She wished she'd thought to bring a warmer jacket. It was a long time since she had been up and about this early in the morning, and she hoped Matt Davenport didn't make a habit of starting work at seven o'clock.

The car slid to a halt exactly in line with the steps, and the driver leapt smartly out to open the passenger door behind him. Flora stopped jigging around and tried to look alert and efficient as a man got out holding a briefcase. She eyed him in some surprise. He was young, with an eager expression. Surely this wasn't the tyrannical Matt Davenport everyone was so scared of?

It wasn't. At that moment another man stepped from the limousine and, even though she had never laid eyes on him before, Flora knew at once that *this* was Matt Davenport. He was tall and dark, and was holding a mobile phone to one ear so that she couldn't see much of his face, but there was no mistaking the power he exuded. It was there in the arrogant set of his shoulders and the forceful stride, in the impatient snap of his fingers to the young man who leapt forward with the briefcase.

'Don't worry, I'll be able to deal with him.' Wasn't that what she had said breezily to Paige only last night? Now she wasn't so sure. If there was any dealing to be done, she had a nasty feeling that Matt Davenport would be the one doing it, not her.

He had stopped briefly to confer with the young man as she watched him, but now turned abruptly and, still talking on the phone, was heading straight to where Flora stood at the foot of the steps. Realising that he was almost upon her, Flora straightened and pinned on her best smile.

He walked straight past her. Flora's jaw dropped. 'Er...Mr Davenport?' she said, hurrying after him.

'Who are you?' He lifted the phone away from his ear but didn't even slacken his pace.

'I'm Flora Mason, your new secretary,' she said a little breathlessly. She was having practically to run to keep up with him, and it was a struggle to keep hold of her bag and hold back the long hair whipping about her face. 'They told me to meet you here.'

Matt Davenport stopped with his foot on the bottom step and lowered the phone. It was hard to tell much about the girl panting along beside him, apart from the fact that she had a lot of hair blowing over her face. He stared at her for one brief, annihilating moment before he continued up the steps.

'Are you the best they could send me?'

'Yes...I mean, they asked me to come for a trial today,' puffed Flora, clambering gamely behind him. 'Paige recommended me,' she added, with more than a hint of desperation. 'She said you just needed someone temporary until she could come back to work.'

Matt stopped so suddenly at the top of the steps that she ran into him. '*You're* Paige's friend?' He couldn't believe that this messy girl could have anything in common with his impeccably neat, discreet and elegant PA.

'Yes.' Flora was flustered by the impact with a body so hard it had driven the breath from her body. She swallowed and made another futile attempt to pull away the hair which had now plastered itself to her lipstick. 'She suggested my name to your personnel department, and they contacted me yesterday.'

Matt favoured her with another hard stare, and then grunted. 'They must have been desperate! You take shorthand?'

'Yes, but—'

'Speak French?'

'Yes.'

'All right,' he said brusquely. 'We'll see how you get on today. It's too late to get anyone else anyway.'

With that he turned into the plane and continued with his phone conversation, completely ignoring the brightly welcoming smile of the flight attendant.

Charming! Flora was beginning to realise why everyone who knew Matt Davenport grimaced when she mentioned his name. Still, she seemed to have passed the first test. She climbed the last step rather wearily and met the sympathetic gaze of the other girl, who mouthed, 'Good luck!' as she moved past her to close the door.

Flora had never been inside a private jet, and she looked about her with interest. It certainly wasn't like any plane she had been in before. Everything was cream-coloured and very clean, and the huge seats were sumptuously upholstered, reeking wealth and comfort. The only thing spoiling the atmosphere of pampered luxury was its owner.

Matt Davenport had chosen a seat facing her, halfway

down the cabin. Now that she wasn't struggling with her
wretched hair, she could see him properly for the first
time. There was something dark and forbidding about
him, and even in an immaculately cut grey suit he looked
too uncompromisingly tough for his surroundings. He
had a stern face, with severe, dark features, and an air
of ruthless determination that was the antithesis of her
own rather frivolous approach to life. It was a shame,
Flora thought, considering his mouth, and she wondered
how different he would look when he smiled. *If* he
smiled.

'Tell him eight million is our last offer,' he was snarling into the phone. He listened for a moment and impatience swept across his face. 'Just do it!' he said, and
snapped the phone shut without a word of farewell.

Looking up, he saw Flora watching him from the
other end of the cabin and his frown deepened. 'You!
What's your name again?'

'Flora Mason.'

'What are you doing hanging around down there?' He
pointed the phone at the seat opposite him. 'Come here
and sit down!'

'Yes, sir!' Flora muttered, but not loud enough for
him to hear.

Matt eyed her, unimpressed, as she made her way
down the aisle. She was obviously no beauty, but she
wouldn't be too bad if she were properly groomed. As
it was, she looked a complete mess, with her hair tangled
about her face and that ridiculously inappropriate outfit
she had on. Look at her, a sleeveless top, that crumpled
cotton jacket and a pink—pink!—skirt that was far
shorter than Paige would ever allow herself to wear! OK,
so she had good legs, but he would have preferred her
in one of Paige's classic grey suits.

He was irritated, too, by the breezy way she plumped
herself down in the seat opposite him. Instead of producing a notebook and waiting neatly, quietly, expec-

tantly for him to speak, she dug around in the bag at her feet before pulling out a hairbrush. Under Matt's astonished eyes, she tipped her head right forward and proceeded to brush the tangles vigorously from her hair.

'That's better,' she said at last, swinging her hair back and away from her face as she lifted her head and smiled at him.

Matt found himself looking into a pair of direct, dancing blue eyes and he was conscious of an odd jolt of surprise. Suddenly she didn't look ordinary at all.

He didn't return her smile. It was almost as if she had caught him unawares, and that wasn't a feeling Matt Davenport was used to. It wasn't one he liked, either, and he frowned. 'I thought Paige told me you were an experienced PA?' he said suspiciously.

Funny, Flora had always thought Americans had lovely warm voices. Matt's was as cold and hard as his glacial green eyes. It was a shame because, with a mouth like that, he really ought to have a voice like warm treacle. Oh, well, it wasn't as if she had to marry the man. All she had to do was put up with him for three months—if she passed this trial today, that was.

'I am,' she told him, sitting up straighter and trying to look like an experienced PA—whatever one of *those* looked like. Anyway, she *was* experienced, Flora reminded herself. It was just that her experience was wide rather than deep.

Matt obviously wasn't convinced. 'You don't look like a top-class PA to me,' he said brutally.

'Well, you know what they say about appearances,' said Flora chattily.

'No,' he said, looking through his briefcase for the note Paige had made for him about her English friend. 'What do they say?'

'You know, how deceptive they can be,' she encouraged him.

He looked up at that. Flora had often wondered how

anyone could really have piercing eyes, but that was exactly what Matt's were like. She felt as if she were being skewered by that cold green gaze.

'They're certainly deceptive if you're trying to tell me that any other company with a professional reputation to maintain has employed you as an assistant at a presidential level,' he said cuttingly. 'Look at you—your hair's a mess, your jacket's all creased and slipping off your shoulder, your skirt's too short, and no PA *I've* ever come across has worn a sleeveless top to work—or shoes as unsuitable as the ones you've got on.'

Flora leant forward. 'Well, you ought to know about appearances being deceptive,' she said. 'Paige told me that you were really very nice and that I'd enjoy working with you!'

For a moment, Matt couldn't quite believe that he'd heard right. Secretaries might quail when he spoke. Some trembled, some wept, but none of them had ever fixed him with a defiant blue stare and answered back!

'She didn't tell me you had a smart mouth,' he said dangerously.

'She didn't tell *me* you had no sense of humour,' Flora retorted before she could help herself, and they glared at each other across the table that divided them.

'Do you want this job or not?' Matt demanded.

Too late, Flora remembered Paige. 'Please, Flora,' her friend had begged when she had rung from the States to say that she wouldn't be coming to London after all. 'Mom's going into hospital next week, and even if things go well she won't be able to manage for at least three months. I can't go over to England and leave her while she's so sick. It'll be OK if I can stay in New York, but Mr Davenport wants to be in London while he sets up this European deal and he's really going to need an assistant.'

'Paige, Elexx is a huge organisation,' said Flora. 'Even I've heard of it. I can't believe its president can't find a secretary! Why don't they just promote someone from the London office temporarily?'

'They *could*,' said Paige somewhat dubiously. She hesitated. 'The thing is, Flora, Matt Davenport isn't the easiest man in the world to work for. Don't get me wrong!' she hurried on before Flora could say anything. 'He's very nice really, but it's true that he can be very...demanding, I suppose. They've tried five girls since he's been in London and they've all been disasters. I think they're getting desperate. In the end, they asked me what I thought, and I suggested they contact you.'

'But, Paige, I don't know anything about all that high-powered stuff you do,' Flora objected.

'You've got all the right secretarial skills,' Paige pointed out. 'You can be perfectly intelligent when you want to be, too! You'd pick things up easily enough. And you speak French fluently—that's really important with this European deal coming up. And, most important of all, you wouldn't be afraid of Mr Davenport. Actually, I think you'd like each other.'

Flora didn't think that was very likely. She couldn't imagine that she would have anything at all in common with a man like Matt Davenport, who was reputedly one of the most ruthless and hard-headed businessmen in the United States.

'There must be any number of highly qualified PAs in London,' she said. 'Why don't they advertise for someone?'

'That's what they'll do unless I can find someone to fill in for me, and that's just it. Lots of top PAs would love my job, but if he gets someone too good he'll get used to her, and then he won't want to change back to me when Mom's better.'

Flora couldn't help grinning down the phone. 'Oh, so you want me to fill in because you know I won't be any good, is that it?' she teased, pretending to take offence.

'Of course not!' said Paige. 'No, it's just...well, I love

my job, Flora, and I don't want to lose it. At least I know you wouldn't want it permanently. You've got too many other things you want to do. I only thought about it after you told me the bank manager wouldn't let you go off travelling until you'd cleared some of your debts. Matt Davenport pays top money, Flora,' she cajoled. 'You could earn enough in three months to buy yourself a round-the-world ticket *and* keep my job safe for me while you're at it. Please say you'll do it!'

Actually, Flora hadn't needed all that much cajoling. Her current erratic run of temporary secretarial work meant that she had barely enough to live on, let alone tackle the overdraft and the looming credit card bill. The thought of paying them both off in one fell swoop had been very appealing, and surely it couldn't be *that* difficult to put up with Paige's difficult boss?

It was just that now she had met Matt Davenport for herself, it didn't seem *quite* as easy as it had when she had breezily assured Paige that she would be fine. Flora eyed him cautiously. He was watching her with a grimly implacable look in his eyes.

Did she want the job? Flora thought of Paige and how grateful she had been, and then she thought about how good it would feel to toss a cheque across the bank manager's desk and jump on the next plane heading to the sun. This was no time for pride and, anyway, the plane was already speeding down the runway, so it was a bit late to ask to get off.

'Yes,' she told him firmly.

'Then I suggest you keep that kind of smart-ass comment to yourself,' he told her with a snap.

'Sorry,' said Flora, hoping she sounded sufficiently contrite. 'It was just that I spent ages with my flatmates trying to decide what to wear last night. I wanted to look smart to go to Paris for the day, and after all the effort we went to it was a bit hard to hear my outfit dismissed out of hand just because it was a bit windy!'

Matt looked across at her in disbelief. 'That's your idea of smart, is it?'

She glanced defensively down at the jacket and suede skirt, both borrowed. Jo was very proud of her skirt, and she had lent it on the strict understanding that it was only for a day and in the higher cause of Flora's glamorous new image as PA to a jet-setting tycoon. She would be furious when she heard what Matt had thought of it! 'It was the best we could do,' Flora told him, pushing her hair behind her ear. 'We can't all afford designer wardrobes, you know.'

'Obviously not.' Almost reluctantly, Matt found himself interested, and he studied Flora across the table. She looked better now that she had brushed her hair, he had to admit. It was, he thought, a nondescript colour, darker than gold but not quite brown, and it fell silkily to her shoulders, neater now, but somehow much too casual. In fact, everything about her was too casual. Minimal make-up, lipstick a patent afterthought, the long brown legs bare. Weren't the British supposed to be uptight and formal? There was absolutely nothing uptight and formal about *this* Brit.

She was attractive enough, he admitted grudgingly to himself, but the stubborn tilt to her chin and the challenging glint in those extraordinary blue eyes spelt trouble in his experience. It was clear that she was quite unsuitable. He wanted someone calm and quiet and efficient to replace Paige, not some wisecracker. There was nothing calm about this Flora or whatever her name was. She had an alert, restless quality that made her at once vivid and vaguely unsettling.

On the other hand, she didn't look the type to burst into tears as soon as he raised his voice, and there was certainly nothing nervous about her. The latest girl the Human Resources Unit had provided had looked so scared whenever he'd walked into the room that she'd given him indigestion. Since Flora was here, he might as well find out a bit more about her.

'You haven't got any top-level experience at all, have you?' he said after a moment.

Flora hesitated. 'No,' she admitted at last. He obviously didn't like her, so she might as well be honest. 'But I think that might be an advantage,' she added bravely.

'How do you work that out?' Matt asked with a sardonic look.

'Well, if I'd worked for a tycoon before I might be tempted to compare you.'

The formidable brows rose in unconscious hauteur. 'Compare me?'

'Yes, you know...' Flora leant forward eagerly. 'I'd spend my whole time saying, Oh, but Mr X only ever buys his private islands in the Caribbean,' she told him, assuming a languidly affected air that sat oddly with the mischief dancing in her blue eyes. 'Or, Mr Y *always* keeps a magnum of champagne chilling in his limousine—and that would really irritate you, wouldn't it?' she finished with an abrupt return to her normal voice.

'It would,' Matt confirmed, amused in spite of himself. He didn't actually smile, but Flora definitely saw one corner of the stern mouth dent a little and felt encouraged. 'I think you've got an odd idea of the reality of working for "tycoons", as you call us. If we spent our whole time swilling champagne and jetting off to private islands, we'd soon lose our grip on our businesses. Paige will tell you that I spend most of my time in the office, and, although she deals with my travel arrangements, she's more likely to spend her day dealing with paperwork than ordering up the private jet!'

'So why do you need someone with senior management level experience?' Flora countered, and he let out an irritable sigh.

'Because,' he said, with an unmistakable edge to his

voice, 'if you'd worked for someone in a similar position, you would know all about the importance of discretion, professionalism and the need both to protect me and represent me to the outside world. It wouldn't do anything for my reputation to have you sitting outside my office. You don't exactly project the right image, do you?'

'Why not?' she said, offended.

'You're too...' Matt waved a dismissive hand as he searched for the right word '...too relaxed,' he decided eventually.

'I'm sure I could poker up and look repressed if I tried,' said Flora with some tartness, and then held her hands up quickly as his brows snapped together. 'Just joking!'

'I don't need a PA who can make jokes,' Matt said in a scathing voice. 'I need someone I can trust to work on sensitive and confidential material, and that means someone efficient, committed and discreet. Nothing you've said to me so far suggests that you possess any of those qualities!'

'You won't know unless you give me a try.' Flora hastened to make amends for her blunder. 'Honestly, I could do the job. I can do shorthand and I can find my way around most word-processing programs. I'm a quick learner and I don't mind hard work—as long as I don't have to do it for more than a few months at a time,' she added with scrupulous honesty. 'But you wouldn't need more than three months, so that wouldn't make any difference to you.'

'And what qualities, other than this extraordinary ability to work for a full three months, do you have to offer me?' asked Matt, not even bothering to hide his sarcasm.

'I speak fluent French,' she pointed out. 'And I speak German, too, but not as well.'

Matt refrained from gasping with wonder. 'What else?'

There was a pause while Flora searched for some other abilities she possessed that might impress him. An ability to enjoy life to the full wouldn't cut much ice with Matt Davenport. She could do cartwheels, poured a mean gin and tonic, and could always be relied upon to get a party going, but somehow she doubted that there would be much scope to display such talents working with him. 'Paige recommended me,' she said at last, driven to the wall.

Even to her own ears it didn't sound very impressive, but it was the only thing she had mentioned that gave Matt pause for thought. Paige had been his personal assistant for the last four years and he respected her judgement. It wasn't like her to recommend someone as unsuitable as Flora appeared to be. There had to be more to this girl than met the eye. Nobody could be quite as frivolous as she seemed, anyway.

He frowned out of the window. 'I wish I had Paige with me now,' he said almost to himself. He hated being distracted by the impossible business of trying to find and then train a replacement for her.

'Well, you can't have her while her mother's sick,' Flora pointed out. 'So you might as well have me instead.'

Matt looked back at her and his eyes narrowed suspiciously. 'Why are you so keen to work for me?'

The blue eyes met his guilelessly. 'I want a short-term job that will earn me as much money as possible,' she said with disarming honesty. 'Paige said you would pay a generous salary,' she added with a hopeful look.

'It's too early to talk about salaries,' he said in a crushing voice. 'The whole point of today is to give you a trial. *If* you can work satisfactorily, and *if* your French is up to scratch, I'll consider taking you on for the three months, but that's all I'm prepared to say at this stage.'

'I won't disappoint you,' said Flora, but Matt only

grunted in an unconvinced way and returned to his papers.

'We'll see,' was all he would say, and she subsided, thinking it might be wiser not to press him any further at this stage. She would just have to show him how good a secretary she could be when she tried. Maybe not as good as Paige, but good enough for three months, surely?

'Would you care for some coffee, Mr Davenport?' The flight attendant was hovering obsequiously.

'Black,' he said without looking up.

'And you, Miss...?'

'Flora,' said Flora firmly. 'And, yes, please, I'd love some coffee,' she went on with exaggerated politeness to make up for Matt's monosyllabic rudeness. 'Just with milk, please. Thank you so much.'

The elaborate reply was not lost on Matt, who cast her a sharp glance as the flight attendant moved away. Flora returned his look innocently and pulled the lever on the arm of the seat to tilt herself back.

'Fantastic plane,' she told him. 'I could fall asleep in a seat like this.'

He eyed her coldly. 'You're not on vacation. You're here to work.'

'Oh, right.' Flora put her seat back into the upright position and dug out a notebook and pen.

Matt barely allowed her time to flick her notebook open before he started. He dictated notes and memos and letters at a punishing speed, and didn't even pause for a thank you when the flight attendant brought them their coffees. Not that Flora had a chance even to sip at hers. Her pen raced over the page while the cup sat tantalisingly beside her, getting colder and colder.

Luckily, his phone rang before she got completely left behind, and he broke off to answer it. Flora gulped at her tepid coffee, waiting until he had finished the conversation so that she could get in quickly before he could start dictating again. 'Can you just tell me exactly what it is we're going to do today?' she pleaded. 'It would make it much easier.'

Matt frowned. 'Weren't you briefed when you were told to come for a trial?' No harm in reminding her that it *was* still a trial.

'Not really. Paige told me that you were involved in some European deal, and when your personnel people rang me up about the arrangements for this morning they just said you were going to Paris for the day.'

'How did you expect to translate for me if you didn't know what we were going to be talking about?' Matt demanded in some exasperation. 'You should have asked before we started.'

'I didn't have a chance,' Flora pointed out. 'That's why I'm asking now.'

'Oh, very well,' he said irritably. He didn't have time for this kind of thing. 'I presume you know what Elexx is about?'

'Electronics,' she said, hoping that he wouldn't ask her for any more details.

Fortunately, her answer seemed to satisfy him and he continued without discovering that Flora had very little idea what electronics meant, let alone what his company did with it. 'Elexx is one of the leading electronics companies in the US at the moment, but we're looking to expand globally. We already have a good hold in the markets around the Pacific Rim, but there's a huge potential market here in Europe and I intend that Elexx gets a share of it.

'It's such an important project that I want to oversee it myself. That's why I'm basing myself in London while we're involved in negotiations and setting up the final deal. There's no reason why I shouldn't do it all from New York, but I like to meet people face to face. That's where you come in.'

'Oh?' said Flora cautiously.

'At the moment we're concentrating on mergers and acquisitions in France,' he told her severely. 'I understand French, but I have to say I don't speak it very well, and I need someone who can take notes from the French and interpret for me if necessary. Can you do that?'

'Of course,' said Flora, who didn't think she knew enough about electronics to talk about them in English, let alone in French. Still, there was no point in telling Matt that at this stage.

In the end, it wasn't nearly as bad as she feared, as the negotiations were about finance and possible locations, and her French was more than adequate for that. She even enjoyed herself, in spite of the fact that for all she saw of Paris they might as well have stayed in London. Matt dictated notes all the way, barely pausing for breath as they landed, and strode across the tarmac to a waiting limousine, throwing orders over his shoulder to Flora, who trotted along behind, trying to keep up and scribble notes at the same time.

She would have liked to have sat back and enjoyed the view as they slid into Paris in the cocooned comfort of the limousine, but Matt had other ideas and simply carried on dictating. Defiantly, Flora snatched a few glances at the familiar blue-grey Parisian streets, but it wasn't worth it when she lost the thread of what he was saying and had to ask him to repeat himself.

By the time they got to the first meeting, Flora was pink in the face with the effort of keeping up with the punishing pace Matt set, and glad of the chance to drop into a chair. While Matt exchanged greetings with the others round the table, she wriggled out of her jacket and hung it behind her, although she soon wished she hadn't. She could feel the contempt emanating from the two other ferociously smart secretaries present, and was suddenly very conscious of the skimpiness of her top.

Matt eyed her with equal disapproval, irritated by the

way her bare arms kept distracting him when he was trying to listen to an important point. Her skin looked warm and inviting, with a golden glow of summer. God only knew what the French thought of him turning up with an assistant who looked as if she had just dropped in on her way to the beach. Her French might be good, but she wasn't doing much for Elexx's image as an efficient, highly professional company at the cutting edge of technology.

Then he saw the way the financial director of the French company was looking at Flora, his eyes travelling appreciatively over her curves. As Matt watched, the Frenchman smiled at Flora, who smiled sunnily back at him, and Matt scowled. 'It would help if you stopped flirting and concentrated on what was going on!' he hissed into her ear. 'And for God's sake, cover yourself up!'

So Flora put her jacket back on and sat getting hotter and hotter. They were in meetings all day, without even time for lunch, she mourned. Typical that the first time she should ever be in Paris with someone rich enough to buy a wonderful meal, they had to make do with coffee and sandwiches in a meeting. Matt obviously wasn't a believer in schmoozing. No time was wasted on small talk; the meeting started as soon as he arrived and they got straight down to business.

By the time they got back to the plane in the early evening, Flora was exhausted. She tottered down the aisle, collapsed untidily into her seat and eased off her shoes with a long sigh. 'That's better!' she said, leaning back and closing her eyes with relief.

Matt, who had been on the point of dictating notes on the last meeting, eyed her with a mixture of irritation and uncharacteristic compunction. She did look tired, he realised, letting his gaze rest on her face. It was easier to look at her when those unsettling blue eyes were

closed, he discovered, easier to notice the curve of her
throat or the sweep of lashes against her cheek.

She had proved herself much more useful than he had
ever imagined when he had first laid eyes on her, Matt
admitted grudgingly to himself. In spite of that scruffy
appearance, she appeared to have some intelligence, and
she had coped with everything he had thrown at her that
day. Her French was excellent, too, and he had noticed
how the French negotiators had responded to her ability
to lighten the atmosphere and dissolve certain tensions
in her translation.

It was a pity she was so...Matt searched for the right
word...so distracting, he decided eventually. He needed
an unobtrusive assistant, one who was there with the
right information when he required it but otherwise
faded into the background. Matt couldn't imagine Flora
fading anywhere. She made him think of sea and sunshine and warmth when he *should* be thinking about pro-
ductivity and profit margins and nothing else.

Matt had always prided himself on his ability to focus
single-mindedly on the subject under discussion, and it
irritated him that a girl like Flora should disturb that
concentration, shimmering at the edge of his awareness
even when she was sitting perfectly still next to him. It
wasn't even as if she were beautiful. Her nose was too
big, her jaw too determined. When her eyes were closed
like this, he could almost persuade himself that she was
no more than ordinary-looking.

It was just that he was suddenly conscious of an inexplicable urge to lean over and smooth those stray hairs
away from her face and let his fingers linger on the
warmth of her skin.

As if she had heard his thoughts, Flora's eyes opened
before Matt had a chance to look away, and he found
himself locked into a dark, intensely blue gaze. A feeling
like a fist closing around his heart gripped him so un-
expectedly that for a long moment he could only stare

back at her, and, when at last he did manage to wrench his eyes away, he was oddly shaken.

The look in the cool green eyes had been so peculiar that Flora touched her fingers tentatively to her mouth. Had she fallen asleep with her mouth open? She didn't seem to have been dribbling, anyway, but why, then, had Matt been looking at her like that? Flora couldn't begin to guess what that look had meant; all she knew was that it had made her heart begin to thud slowly and uncomfortably against her ribs.

'I think I must have nodded off,' she said at last, to break the suddenly constrained silence. 'It's been a long day.'

'You'll have to get used to these hours if you want to work for me,' said Matt gruffly.

Flora's face lit up as she realised what he had said. 'You mean I've got the job?'

Matt was irritated with himself for not knowing whether he wanted her to work for him or not. Hadn't he just decided that she was too distracting? But she had worked hard today and, although he had pushed her harder than was perhaps fair, he hadn't heard her complain once. And then there was the fact that there was no one else, unless they advertised outside the company, and that might take weeks...

'If you want it, and think you can do it,' he said.

Flora's smile was dazzling with relief. 'You won't regret it,' she promised him.

Matt wasn't so sure.

CHAPTER TWO

MATT made himself look away from Flora's face and out of the window, but it was as if her smile were imprinted on his eyes. It danced still on the clouds, on the wing flashing silver in the evening sun, and when he looked down instead, at the papers on the desk, it glimmered there too, in spite of his efforts to blink it away.

'How do you know Paige?' he asked Flora abruptly. Paige had been with him four years. She was the best PA he had ever had, but she was so self-effacing that he knew virtually nothing about her. When he tried to conjure up her image, all he got was Flora's face, with her eyes full of sunshine. 'You're not at all alike.'

'No,' Flora agreed. She undid her seat belt and tucked her legs up underneath her like a little girl. 'Paige is incredibly calm and patient—but then you must know that.' You would have to be patient to last four years as Matt Davenport's PA, she reflected, but didn't say so.

It was obvious that Matt knew perfectly well what she meant, though. 'I do know it,' he said dryly.

'She's disgustingly well organised, too,' Flora went on hastily. 'We all used to wish we could hate her, but we never could. She's just too nice.'

'We?'

'There was a whole crowd of us at university together. Paige came over on an exchange year. She was studying French, like me. We lived in the same hall of residence and we've stayed in touch ever since.'

Matt regarded her thoughtfully. It all sounded reasonable enough, but it was hard to imagine the poised and elegant Paige having much in common with a girl like

Flora. Still, she must have thought that Flora had something to recommend her. 'Paige seemed very keen for me to give you a trial,' he said. 'Why was that?'

'She knows that I'm not interested in a permanent job,' said Flora cautiously. It seemed unlikely that Paige would have confessed her worries about being replaced to Matt, and she didn't want to betray a confidence. 'I'd told her that I was desperate to earn some money to pay off some of my debts, so, when she knew that she wouldn't be coming with you, she thought I'd be the ideal person to replace her temporarily.'

'"Ideal" isn't the word I would have chosen,' said Matt, with a sardonic look.

'You know what I mean,' she said, brushing the detail aside as unimportant. 'You've got to fill a well-paid post for three months, and I need a job that pays well for three months. You need someone who speaks French; I speak French.' She spread her hands expressively. 'We're made for each other, darling!' she joked.

There was an odd little silence. Flora was sure she could hear her words echoing around the cabin...*made for each other...made for each other, darling...*' What a stupid thing to say! When would she learn to think before she opened her mouth? He would think she was absolutely ridiculous.

Almost unwillingly, her eyes met Matt's. The cool green gaze was quite unreadable, but Flora felt a blush stealing up her cheeks and she tucked her hands away under the table. 'In a manner of speaking,' she added lamely.

'I take your point,' said Matt, with a dryness that only deepened her flush. 'Why aren't you looking for a permanent position if you've got all these skills that make you so "ideal"?'

'I've never found a job I'd want to commit myself to for more than a few months,' said Flora. 'Temping can be a bit dreary sometimes, but I like not knowing where

I'll be, and, even if it turns out to be an awful job, I know that I can walk away at the end of the week.

'Anyway,' she told him, 'what I really want to do is to travel. I've had a great time in London, but I'm ready to see the rest of the world now. Unfortunately, my bank manager doesn't agree. He says I'm not going anywhere until I've paid off my overdraft and credit card.'

Flora brooded for a moment, remembering that interview at the bank. Matt probably had no idea just how condescending and brutally practical bank managers could be. *He* would never be summoned to the bank to discuss his overdraft. He could ask to borrow millions and the bank would fall over itself to lend him the money, although she needed a loan so much more than he did. Sometimes life just wasn't fair.

'So you're planning to save this enormous salary you think I'm going to pay you?' said Matt, which Flora didn't think sounded very encouraging. Never mind, an enormous salary to her would probably seem pitiful to him, and she would surely be earning more than she had been at the temping agency.

'That's the idea,' she said. 'Not that I've ever been very good at saving,' she went on a little glumly. 'But this time I've got a specific plan in mind, so it should be easier.'

'And what exactly is this plan?'

'I've told you, I want to travel.'

'Yes, but where?' asked Matt, impatient as always with vague ideas.

'Everywhere!' she told him, and he sighed.

'That sounds specific!' he said acidly.

Flora ignored the disparagement in his tone. 'But it's true!' she said. Her hands escaped up into the air once more to gesture expansively and she leant forward, blue eyes alight with enthusiasm

'I want to see everything! There's a whole world out there just waiting for me. I've only ever travelled in

Europe, and I want to see something different. I want to hack my way through jungles and bounce across deserts in dusty Land Rovers. I want to lie on a hot white beach and listen to coconuts drop. I want to watch a giraffe run in the wild. I want new tastes, new smells—'

She stopped, seeing the dismissive expression on Matt's face. 'I suppose you think I'd be better off settling down with a "proper job", as my bank manager calls it?' she said with a touch of defensiveness.

Matt shrugged, unwilling to admit that he envied her the zest and enthusiasm that had lit her face as she talked. 'I think you're a romantic,' he said, making it sound like an insult.

Deflated, Flora sat back with a sigh. 'That's what Seb says.'

'Who's Seb?'

'My boyfriend—or, rather, my ex-boyfriend,' she corrected herself darkly. 'We'd been going out together since university, but we argued so much about travelling that in the end we decided we were better off just being friends. Seb couldn't see the point of taking a couple of years off just to see the world,' she went on when Matt said nothing. 'He's very ambitious, and he thinks it's madness to take off when you should be trying to establish yourself in a career.'

'He sounds a sensible man,' said Matt, although part of him wondered why a man would prefer to be 'just friends' with a girl like Flora.

'You would say that,' said Flora crossly, forgetting whom she was talking to. 'You and Seb can concentrate on your work, if that's what you want to do, but I want to live a little! I was a bit disappointed when he insisted on staying in London, but now I think I'm much better off on my own.'

Matt looked out of the window. 'So you're unattached at the moment?'

'Until I can find someone who's prepared to give up

everything to come with me,' she said. 'And I don't think that's very likely somehow.'

'I'm glad to hear it,' said Matt.

Flora's heart did an odd somersault and landed back in place with a thud that left her stupidly breathless. 'Oh?' she said weakly. 'Why's that?'

'I need my assistant to stay in the office for as long as she's needed, and to be able to drop everything to come on trips like this at short notice without some boyfriend complaining that she's always late or getting jealous about the amount of time we spend together,' he said dismissively. 'I want my PA to be able to concentrate on me without any distractions at home. If you work for me, Flora, I expect to be your number one priority.'

What had she thought? That he would want her for her blue eyes? Ridiculous disappointment gripped Flora by the throat, and, desperate in case it showed in her face, she lifted her chin and looked directly into Matt's eyes. 'Paying off my overdraft so that I can travel is my number one priority,' she said recklessly. 'You can be my number two priority.'

Taken aback, Matt stared at her, and Flora quailed inwardly, certain that this time she had gone too far, but after a nerve-racking moment of utter silence he surprised her by laughing. 'You've got a nerve, Flora, I'll give you that!'

It was Flora's turn to be taken aback. Actually, she was more than taken aback. Stunned would be a better description of how she felt when she saw how completely laughter transformed him, dissolving the hard look in the cool green eyes and creasing his face into dangerously intriguing lines. His teeth were very white and very strong, and his smile was warm with such devastating, unexpected charm that Flora felt the air evaporate around her, leaving her gasping for breath.

'I'm just being honest,' she croaked.

Matt's smile still lurked unnervingly as he watched her across the table. 'OK,' he said. 'You work as hard as you did today until Paige gets back, and I'll take the number two slot.'

Flora drew a deep, steadying breath. It was only a smile, after all. There was absolutely no reason for her heart to cartwheel crazily around her chest like that. 'It's—' She broke off, appalled at the squeak in her voice and cleared her throat. 'It's a deal.'

Twenty-five past eight. Flora checked her watch again, hardly able to believe that she had made it to the office in Mayfair in time.

'Be there at half-past eight,' Matt had said by way of farewell when they got off the plane the night before. He had stopped to glance back at Flora, whose feet had been killing her, as she negotiated the last step with a grimace. 'Oh, and do something about your hair,' he had added as a brusque afterthought, and then he had walked off towards the waiting car without another word, leaving Flora alone and rather forlorn on the tarmac.

Not that she had stayed forlorn for long, she reminded herself hastily, straightening her shoulders and walking across the imposing reception area to the lifts. She had shaken off the feeling as soon as he had gone. She had got the job; that was the main thing! In three months' time she would have paid off her debts and the world would be her oyster. She wasn't going to let anything divert her from that!

Now, Flora stood in the lift carrying her up to the president's office and examined her reflection in the mirror rather dubiously. It had taken her hours to tie her hair back in a French plait this morning, but somehow it didn't look as smart on her as it did on other girls. Still, it would just have to do, she told herself, hoping that Matt wouldn't notice quite how crooked everything looked.

After his trenchant comments about her outfit yesterday, she had put on a long, soft brown skirt and a plain short-sleeved shirt. She looked dull and horribly prim, Flora thought, but neat—well, neat*ish*—and at least Matt wouldn't be able to complain that she was dressed inappropriately today.

To her surprise, there was no sign of Matt when she found the door marked 'President's Office'. Inside, all was hushed and quiet. The office she stepped into was so palatial that she thought at first that it must be Matt's, until she saw the desk guarding a door into an inner office and realised that this was *her* room! It was dauntingly uncluttered. To Flora, used to temping in noisy, open-plan offices, having a room of her own to work in was unbelievable luxury.

Flora hung her bag on a hook and sat down at the desk, running her hand over the polished wood and pulling open the drawers. Each slid silently open to reveal its disconcertingly well-organised contents. Flora shut the last and turned her attention to the array of electronic equipment, half of which she didn't even recognise. She would worry about that when she came to it, she decided with characteristic optimism, and bounced experimentally up and down on the chair instead, approving its cushioned comfort.

This was the life! No more spreadsheets or databases, no more dreary filing. No more standing by a drinks machine for weak cups of coffee. For the next three months she would be working in the lap of luxury. This might be her one chance to see how the other half lived *and* to earn enough to go off and do some living of her own! Exultant at the prospect, Flora stretched out her arms and spun herself round in the chair with a whoop of joy.

Matt chose that moment to walk in the door. He had been irritated to discover that Flora's image had lingered at the edges of his mind the whole of the previous eve-

ning, and that just when he'd thought he had succeeded
in banishing it entirely he'd found himself remembering
the blueness of her eyes, the silky tumble of her hair or
the shape of her knees. By the time he walked into the
office he was in a thoroughly bad mood, which was not
improved by the shock of seeing Flora, spinning gaily
on the chair, and altogether more vivid than his memories of her. She had a presence which was somehow
impossible to ignore.

Flora caught sight of Matt as she spun past, and she
dropped her feet hurriedly to bring the chair to a jarring
halt. At least, that was the reason she gave to herself for
the way her heart jolted as she saw him staring incredulously across the room at her.

'Hello,' she said weakly, and then, like a fool, she
blushed. Had he seen her whizzing round on the chair?
To cover her confusion, she got to her feet.

'Oh, it's you,' said Matt by way of a greeting. He felt
oddly taken aback. His first impression had been that
she was just the same as he remembered, only more so,
but now he could see that she had plaited her hair away
from her face, and that she was wearing a long skirt and
a demure blouse cinched neatly together with a belt. She
didn't look smart, Matt decided, but at least she was
more appropriately dressed today.

The direct blue eyes were exactly the same, though,
and so was that jaunty set of her head. And it wasn't
really her fault if the long skirt only made him remember
her legs all the more clearly, or if the severe hairstyle
emphasised the line of her throat and left him with a
vague sense of regret.

It wasn't Flora's fault, Matt knew logically, but it
didn't stop him blaming her, and the knowledge that he
was being unreasonable only exacerbated his bad mood.
'What were you doing on that chair?' he demanded
brusquely.

'I wasn't doing anything,' Flora tried to excuse herself. 'I was just...seeing how it worked.'

'If you want to see how things work, switch on the computer!' snapped Matt as he strode towards his office. 'Or, better still, bring in your notebook. I want to dictate some letters before the phones start ringing.'

Flora eyed him uncertainly. 'What, now?'

'Yes, now!' he snarled. 'When did you think?'

'Wouldn't you like a cup of coffee before you start?' she asked hopefully, but Matt only scowled.

'No,' he said. 'This is an office, not a café. If I want a coffee, I'll ask for one. And if I want you in my office ready to take dictation, I'll ask for that—which, in case you didn't notice, is what I just did!'

Flora suppressed a sigh. 'Right,' she said, and hunted through the desk drawers for a notebook and pen.

By the time she had found them, and presented herself in Matt's room, he was sitting at his desk and ready to start work. He barely gave her time to flip open her notebook before he started dictating.

'Hang on a minute,' said Flora a few minutes later. Her hand already had cramp and he was speaking so fast that it was impossible for her to keep up with him.

Matt waited with bad grace, drumming his fingers impatiently on the desktop while his eyes rested broodingly on Flora. Her head was bent over her notebook as she scribbled notes to remind herself what all her erratic shorthand squiggles had been meant to represent.

He wished he couldn't remember how her hair had looked falling loose to her shoulders. And that shirt she was wearing was all very prim and proper, but it didn't make it any easier to forget how revealingly her top had clung to her yesterday...

'OK.' Flora looked up to find Matt watching her with a peculiarly unfocused expression. He didn't seem to have registered her comment, so she waved her hand to attract his attention. 'I'm ready to go on,' she explained patiently.

Matt looked at her blankly for a moment, and then abruptly snapped back into full consciousness as he realised what he had been thinking about. To make matters worse, he had completely lost the train of what he had been saying. He couldn't even remember what the letter had been about.

'You'll have to read back the last couple of sentences,' he snapped, furious with himself. 'And try to keep up in future!'

He relieved his temper by dictating a sheaf of letters at high speed, and Flora was exhausted by the time he finally let her go. 'Those Paris letters are urgent,' he said as his parting shot. 'I want to sign them as soon as you've done them, and you can fax them straight away.'

Flora wanted to ask why, if they were so urgent, he had spent all that time on those other letters, but she decided on reflection to keep quiet. She was going to keep her head down, keep her mouth closed, and not let Matt Davenport rile her. Think of the money, she told herself. Think of blue lagoons and a hot wind soughing through the coconut palms. Think of what it's going to be like when you get on that plane.

Matt watched, scowling, as Flora got up in what he considered an unnecessarily leisurely way. 'I said *urgent*,' he said pointedly.

'What do you want me to do?' she asked, instantly forgetting her pious resolve. 'Sprint to the door?'

'Some indication that you knew the meaning of "urgent" might be nice!'

'Urgent means that I start typing without finding a cup of coffee first,' said Flora sourly. 'I may die of thirst in the meantime, but what does a little thing like that matter if your faxes arrive thirty seconds earlier?'

'You'll die of something else if you don't get a move

on!' said Matt in exasperation, but Flora was gone, and he was left staring at the door in disbelief.

He had never had a secretary like her before, and he was irritated by the way she seemed to get under his skin. None of his previous assistants had looked like her, none of them had spoken to him the way she did, and certainly none of them had ever acted like her! None of *them* had left him not knowing whether he wanted to laugh or to bang the table in fury, and Matt wasn't at all sure he knew how to deal with the fact that Flora most definitely did.

Matt suddenly realised that he had been glaring at the door for a good five minutes. For Pete's sake, why was he wasting his time thinking about his secretary? He had much more important things to do with his time than wonder about a girl who would only be working for him for a matter of weeks—and much less than that if she didn't learn to keep her smart-ass comments to herself!

Pulling a financial report towards him, Matt opened it with a savage flick and applied himself to the business of putting Flora out of his mind.

Meanwhile, Flora herself was bitterly remembering what Paige had said. 'Matt Davenport isn't the easiest man in the world to work for.'

'Hah!' Flora snorted to herself as she snapped on the computer. Why hadn't she remembered Paige's genius for understatement before she had agreed to take her place as Matt's PA? Matt was rather more than *not easy*. Nice smile or not, he was selfish, unreasonable and generally extremely *difficult*!

It took her a little while to familiarise herself with the word-processing program, but she was banging crossly away at the keyboard when Matt snatched open his door. 'Haven't you finished yet?' he demanded.

Flora was very aware of him looming in the doorway, but she refused to look up from the screen. 'Not quite,' she said through gritted teeth.

'''Not quite''? What does *not quite* mean?'

'It means that I've finished the first letter, have just started the second and still have five to do,' said Flora tightly. 'Damn!' she muttered under her breath as, distracted by Matt prowling around the room, she made a mistake. Jabbing at the 'delete' key, she went back too far, which did nothing to improve her temper.

'What have you been doing?' Matt grumbled. 'I thought you'd have finished them all by now! If Paige had been here, they would all have been typed, signed, faxed and sitting on the right desks in Paris by now!'

'Even Paige can't type at the speed of light!' said Flora, stung. 'I'm going as fast as I can.'

Matt's pacing brought him back to her desk. He picked up the letter she had printed out and studied it in frowning silence, unreasonably annoyed to discover that there was not a single typing error. He couldn't even criticise the layout. Balked, he took a pen from his jacket pocket and scrawled his signature at the bottom of the page.

'I suppose *I* may as well send this,' he said with heavy sarcasm. 'At least that way I know one letter will have arrived.'

Flora set her teeth. 'That would help,' she said.

Matt glared for a moment, then strode over to the fax machine, shoved the paper into the feeder and stabbed out a number. Paige would never have dreamed of letting him do this, he reflected with obscure resentment. It was years since he had had to send his own fax!

Forced to wait while the machine clicked and whirred, he gazed morosely across the room at Flora, who sat typing and apparently ignoring him completely. The sunshine pouring through the window beside her struck the light in her not quite brown hair, suffusing it with gold, and he found himself remembering once more how it had tumbled loose to her shoulders. It was the kind of hair you wanted to pick up and rub through your fingers to see if it was as silky as it looked.

The beep of the fax machine spitting out the letter beside him brought Matt abruptly out of his reverie, and he jerked his eyes away from Flora, furious with himself for letting his mind drift towards her again.

Swinging round, he scowled out of the window instead. Why did Paige's mother have to fall sick right now? He missed his PA's quiet elegance, her air of calm efficiency and discretion. There was something soothing about Paige, while Flora somehow set the air jangling just by sitting there.

'Well?' he barked over his shoulder. 'Have you done any more yet?'

Flora threw his back a venomous glance as she clicked the 'print' button. 'Nearly,' she said with careful control.

Matt couldn't stand still. He paced around the office, stopping every now and then to loom over Flora's shoulder and ask her if she was ready, until the only thing Flora was ready for was to hit him. 'What's taking so long?' he demanded at last.

'I might be able to get on a bit faster if you stopped prowling around and asking me if I've finished every ten seconds!' she snapped, exasperated. 'It's driving me potty!'

If she hadn't been so cross, Flora would have laughed at Matt's expression. He looked positively perplexed. Hadn't anyone ever told him how irritating he was before?

'It doesn't bother Paige,' he said after a moment.

'Well, it bothers *me*,' said Flora through set teeth. 'I will bring you the remaining letters as soon as I have finished them—and that will be a lot sooner if you'll just go away and leave me alone!' She turned back to her notebook. 'You can bring me a cup of coffee if you've got nothing better to do than stand around and hassle me!' she added tartly, but without looking up.

She hadn't meant it seriously, but Matt turned on his heel and strode out of the room, muttering under his breath. Probably gone off to tell the accounts department, or whatever pretentious name it had now, to stop her pay before she had even earned any, Flora thought as she crashed away at the keyboard.

Well, let him! He was impossible, anyway. After a morning like this, it would be a relief to be sacked! She might not earn as much if she went back to temping, but at least she would get a cup of coffee and be treated like a human being.

When Matt came back into the room, Flora deliberately kept her eyes fixed on the screen. She wasn't about to gratify him by showing any interest in his movements. The next instant a cup and saucer were set down beside the keyboard, where she couldn't avoid seeing them, and her fingers stopped in mid-air.

'Your coffee, ma'am,' said Matt's voice, heavy with sarcasm.

Flora stared at the cup and then she lifted her eyes slowly. Matt was watching her, as if perplexed by his own gesture, and her anger evaporated as if it had never been. Maybe he wasn't that impossible after all! She guessed it was a very long time since Matt had had to find his own drink, and the thought of him hunting around the office for a coffee machine tickled her sense of humour.

'Thank you,' she said, trying not to laugh, but Matt saw the amusement lurking in the deep blue eyes.

'What's so funny?' he asked, oddly defensively. He didn't know what had prompted him to go and find Flora some coffee, and he was beginning to wish he hadn't bothered.

'Nothing...I was just imagining you making the coffee, that's all. I don't suppose you do it all that often.'

'I had to ask some girl in the Corporate Development Unit where I could find some,' Matt found himself admitting. 'She looked at me as if I'd beamed down from outer space. Anyone would think no one had ever asked her for coffee before. I felt a complete fool!'

Flora couldn't help laughing then. 'Well, I appreciate it,' she said.

'It was the only way I could think of to shut you up about the coffee,' said Matt gruffly, and then he made the mistake of looking into her eyes. They were warm and blue and dancing with laughter, and somehow he found himself smiling back.

For a long moment the air seemed to tighten and vibrate between them, and then both looked away at the same time. Conscious of a strange sense of constraint, Flora cleared her throat.

'Er...I've finished those letters. This is the last one printing out now.'

'Good.' Matt's brusqueness disguised an inexplicable feeling of dissatisfaction at the way the warmer atmosphere between them had been broken. He placed his hands on Flora's desk and leant on them as he tried to concentrate on reading through the letters she had indicated.

Flora found herself looking down at the hand that lay closest to her own. She felt as if she had never seen a man's hand before. The sleeves of his shirt were rolled casually up his forearm and she could see the creases at his knuckles, the texture of his skin, the way the fine dark hairs grew at his wrist, and she was suddenly gripped by an overwhelming sense of his maleness. All at once it seemed that Matt was no longer her boss, no longer a successful businessman, but simply a man with a physical presence that dried the breath in her throat and set something stirring deep inside her.

His little finger was only millimetres away from her own. If she stretched her hand just a fraction, they would touch. Flora could almost see the electricity sizzling across the tiny space that separated her finger from

Matt's, could almost feel how it would jolt through her if her flesh so much as grazed against his, but the temptation to do just that was so great that she snatched her hand away completely with a tiny gasp that made Matt look up with a frown.

'What's the matter?'

'Nothing,' said Flora quickly. Horrified by the bizarre compulsion to touch him, she pushed back her chair. 'I'll…er…I'll start faxing those letters,' she said. 'After all, I know how urgent they are.'

'Oh…yes.' Matt looked momentarily blank, as if he had forgotten all about the urgency he had insisted on earlier. He signed the last letter, handed it to Flora and stepped away from the desk almost reluctantly. 'I'll leave you to carry on, then.'

There were three phones on Flora's desk, and they rang all morning. Matt had told her that he didn't want to be disturbed, and was closeted in his office, so she was kept busy fielding calls, dealing with faxes, taking messages, checking diaries and working her way through the long list of things to do that Matt had dictated earlier that morning. Paige had sent copious notes to help her, but it still took some time to find out how everything worked.

By lunch-time, having barely had a moment to draw breath, Flora was beginning to feel distinctly frazzled. She hadn't realised how late it was until the door opened and a girl came in. She was tall and very thin, with huge eyes and exquisite cheekbones. Her blonde hair fell in carefully arranged disorder, and she exuded a kind of sultry glamour that made Flora feel lumpish, dull and horribly conscious of her own prim blouse and drearily sensible skirt.

She also seemed vaguely familiar, but as Flora had one phone to her ear, another on her shoulder and a third on hold while she hunted through a sheaf of papers, she didn't waste much time in trying to work out why.

Instead, she watched incredulously as the other girl sank
into one of the armchairs as if she was exhausted.

'Tell Matt I'm here, would you?' she said carelessly.

'Please,' Flora muttered to herself as she put yet another conversation on hold. 'Matt's asked not to be disturbed,' she said as pleasantly as she could. 'Is he expecting you?'

'Of course.' The other girl's eyes flicked dismissively
over Flora, who stiffened, resenting the way one look
could make her feel at least three stone heavier than she
was.

She set her teeth. 'Who shall I say is here?'

There was a tiny pause. 'Just tell him it's me,' said
the girl, in a voice that was edged with steel.

Me? Fine, thought Flora, fed up. She buzzed Matt on
the intercom. 'Me is here to see you,' she said.

'What are you talking about?' he asked irritably.

'You have a visitor, apparently called Me,' Flora explained, with the air of one washing her hands of all
responsibility.

Matt gave an exasperated sigh. 'I suppose you mean
Venezia,' he said. 'Why can't you just say so?'

Flora opened her mouth to point out that she wasn't
a mind-reader, but he had already broken the connection.
At least that explained why the other girl looked vaguely
familiar. Venezia Hobbs was tipped as the new face for
the fashion magazines, although from all Flora had ever
read in the papers she seemed to spend as much time
socialising as she did modelling. It probably also explained the frosty reaction when Flora had asked her
name. Oh, well, Flora thought, not without some satisfaction. It wouldn't do Venezia any harm to realise that
not everyone recognised her. She wasn't *that* famous, in
spite of her pretentious name.

Matt appeared as Flora picked up the phones and tried
to remember who was on which line, but it was hard to
concentrate on her conversation when she had to watch

Venezia unfold her impossibly long legs and stand up to kiss Matt full on the lips. Flora's eyes narrowed. There was no need for Venezia to wind herself around him quite that closely, was there? She would strangle Matt if she wasn't careful. Not that Matt was exactly struggling to get free, Flora noted sourly.

In fact, Matt returned Venezia's extravagant greeting in a rather perfunctory way. Over her shoulder, he could see Flora talking on the telephone, but something in her disparaging blue gaze made him step back from Venezia's embrace.

'Did you book that table?' he asked Flora, brusquely breaking into her conversation.

Flora apologised to her caller and put him on hold yet again. 'What table?'

'At Le Sanglier,' he said impatiently. 'One o'clock.'

She flicked quickly through her notebook, but she was pretty sure she knew nothing about any lunch. 'You didn't mention anything about booking a table.'

'I did,' Matt contradicted her.

'You didn't.'

Matt was beginning to get angry. '*I did*. I've known about this lunch since last week.'

'I'm *so* sorry,' Flora apologised with mock humility. 'Didn't I mention that I failed my telepathy exam?'

'Don't be smart, Flora,' he snapped. 'I've already warned you about that mouth of yours. If you haven't booked it, you'd better ring the restaurant now and tell them we're on our way.'

Flora threw a harassed look at the occupied phones, their receivers laid out in a line on the desk. 'Are you sure you wouldn't prefer a sandwich in the park?' she sighed. 'It's a lovely day.'

Matt's brows snapped together, but before he could bite her head off Venezia entered the conversation. 'Matt, darling, I can't eat sandwiches,' she told him in alarm. 'You know I'm allergic to gluten.'

Flora rolled her eyes, half exasperated, half diverted by Venezia's serious response to her joke, only to find that Matt was watching her. Their eyes met for a fleeting moment, and she was almost sure that she saw a mixture of amusement and impatience in his expression that matched her own.

'In that case, I'd better make sure you get a table,' she said with an ironic look, and then glanced at Matt again. Le Sanglier was one of the most exclusive restaurants in the city, and she didn't think it would be the kind of place that could fit in a last-minute reservation. 'If they're full, do you want me to try somewhere else?'

'No.' If that glimpse of shared amusement had ever existed, it had gone from Matt's eyes now. 'Tell them to find an extra table. I'm not hanging around here while you call half the restaurants in London.'

He stalked out with Venezia wound around his arm, and Flora was left muttering under her breath. How arrogant could you get? Most people had to reserve at least six months in advance to get a table at Le Sanglier. As she dialled the number, she hoped that they would refuse to fit Matt in, but to her disappointment one of the best tables magically became free as soon as she mentioned his name. He might not have been in London very long, but his reputation had preceded him from the States, and they knew already that the name Davenport meant serious money.

It was all right for some, Flora grumbled to herself, ringing back all the people she had had to cut off in order to call the restaurant. What was the point of taking someone as thin as Venezia out to lunch, anyway? She would just toy with a lettuce leaf, or perhaps a piece of raw carrot if she was feeling self-indulgent. About as much fun as feeding a rabbit, Flora decided sourly. Less, probably. At least a rabbit was cuddly. Venezia was about as cuddly as a stick insect—but then, Matt obviously liked his women angular.

Looking down at her own generous curves, Flora suppressed a sigh and went back to work.

'Why don't you have a proper lunch?'

She turned the computer screen off at the button.
'Because if I'm lucky I get time to eat at all, let alone anything else. Besides, it's good for me. I'm going on a diet.' Flora dropped the empty pot into my desk drawer.

CHAPTER THREE

FLORA had never worked as hard in her life as she did over the next two weeks. At least having no time for lunch was good for her figure, she consoled herself, and what with running up the escalators at the tube station every morning in order to get to the office before Matt she was getting positively trim!

Matt walked into the office one day to find her spooning yoghurt with one hand and scrolling through a computer file with the other. He scowled. Really, Flora had the most bizarre ideas of how to behave in an office! She was always kicking off her shoes, gossiped with anyone who came into the office and never seemed in the least perturbed when he caught her calling her friends. And if the word 'sir' had ever passed her lips, Matt had never heard it! When he had pointed out that that was how Paige—not to mention the rest of his staff—addressed him, Flora had merely laughed and reminded him that he was in England now.

'We use first names here,' she had told him gaily. 'I don't see why I should call you sir unless you're prepared to call me madam!'

She was totally unsuitable, Matt told himself irritably. If he had any sense he would have sacked her by now, and yet, in spite of her frivolous, not to say impertinent, attitude to the importance of her position, Flora had proved surprisingly efficient.

Matt was thinking of that as he eyed the yoghurt with disfavour. 'What *is* that you're eating?' he asked.

'My lunch.' Flora scraped out the pot and licked the spoon hungrily. 'Low-fat yoghurt. Revolting.'

'Why don't you have a proper lunch?'

She aimed the empty yoghurt pot at the bin and lobbed it in. 'I'm lucky if I get time to eat a yoghurt, let alone anything else. Besides, it's good for me. I'm going to a ball in a few weeks and I'll never get into my dress unless I lose some weight.'

'You look fine to me,' grunted Matt, who had spent the last two weeks trying not to notice what a contrast Flora's pleasantly rounded figure, with its suggestion of softness and warmth, made to the painful thinness of girls like Venezia. 'At least I know now why you're always so grumpy in the afternoons. It's not surprising if this is all you have to eat all day.'

'I am not always grumpy in the afternoons!'

'Yes, you are,' he contradicted her. 'I hardly dare come out of my room sometimes! Look, I'm going to have lunch now,' he went on gruffly. 'Why don't you come with me? We've got a lot to get done this afternoon, and I'd rather have you in a good mood.'

'I can't go out to lunch,' protested Flora. 'I've got too much to do.'

'There's nothing that can't wait an hour,' said Matt, as surprised as she was by his invitation, and now taken aback by how much he wanted her to come. 'You're still hungry, aren't you?'

'Starving,' she admitted, and in no time at all found herself sitting in a restaurant not far from the office, her mouth watering at the menu even as her eyes goggled at the prices.

It was all too tempting to resist, and Flora threw her diet to the winds as she ordered and then spread butter lavishly on a warm roll. After all, it wasn't every day you were taken out for a meal in a place like this, so she had better make the most of it. Who said there was no such thing as a free lunch?

Matt watched her with some amusement. It made a nice change to see a girl really enjoying her food. His eyes rested on Flora's face as she reached for another roll. He had taken Venezia Hobbs out to dinner the night before, and had been left with a vague feeling of dissatisfaction. Venezia had undeniable glamour, but several times during the meal Matt had been conscious of a creeping sense of boredom. Flora might not be able to hold a candle to Venezia when it came to beauty, sophistication or sheer sex appeal, but Matt couldn't imagine her ever boring him. Infuriating him, yes. Distracting, exasperating and provoking him, certainly, but *boring* him? No, he didn't think so.

Flora, happily chewing her roll, was looking around the room, but when her gaze returned to Matt she found him watching her with such an odd expression in his eyes that she put the roll back down onto her plate uncertainly. For some reason, the silence was suddenly constrained and, unable to look back at him directly, Flora cast around desperately for something to say.

'How's the sightseeing going?' was the best she could come up with, and Matt's dark brows lifted.

'Sightseeing?'

'I was reading about you in the paper on the tube last night,' Flora explained. 'There was a whole piece in the gossip page about how you'd moved to London and how Venezia Hobbs was showing you around.' She glanced at him. 'I think they meant the night-life, but I had this image of her trotting you around the Tower and past Buckingham Palace!'

'I saw those sights a long time ago,' said Matt dryly. 'What else did the paper say?'

'There was rather a lot about how rich and eligible you were, and a few heavy hints about your relationship with Venezia.' Flora's blue eyes gleamed with mischief. 'They say she's the reason you moved to London.'

Matt snorted. 'Why waste your time reading garbage like that?'

'I was just doing some research,' she said. 'I ought to know something about the man I'm working for!'

'You won't learn anything about me in the papers,' said Matt shortly. 'If you want to know anything about me, I suggest you ask me yourself rather than relying on gossip!'

'OK,' said Flora. 'Is it true you're going to move in with Venezia?'

'No, it most definitely isn't!' He cast her a suspicious glance, but Flora's face was the picture of innocence. 'I am living in a hotel suite and that's where I'm staying until we can close the European deal.'

'Why don't you rent a house or something? It would be much nicer than living in a hotel for six months.'

Matt shrugged. 'The hotel suits me. It's not worth moving into a house when I'll be going back to New York at the end of the year.'

Flora watched the waiter pour her a glass of wine. 'Is New York home for you?'

For some reason Matt seemed to be thrown by the question. 'I guess so,' he said. 'That's where the Elexx headquarters are.'

'Yes, but where do you live?'

'I have an apartment in Manhattan, near the office. My mother lives on Long Island—that's where I grew up—so I go there most weekends.'

'It sounds wonderful,' sighed Flora. 'Weekends on Long Island! I'll bet it's a lovely house, too?'

Matt thought of the mansion on the shore, of the swimming pools and the tennis courts and the fleet of staff needed to keep it going. 'It's much too big,' he said. 'Certainly too big for two. My father died when I was eight, so it was just my mother and I.'

Flora thought it sounded sad. 'Were you lonely?'

'Nobody gets a chance to be lonely when my mother's around,' said Matt with a wry smile. 'She loves giving parties and the house was always full of people.'

'Being lonely isn't always the same as being alone,' said Flora gently, and he shot her a look.

'You're right,' he said. 'For me, being alone is a luxury.' He looked down into his glass, swirling the wine absently. 'I bought a ranch in Montana a few years ago. There's plenty of space to be alone there. I like to just get on a horse and ride towards the horizon. It's the only place I feel really free.' He lifted his eyes to Flora as if the thought had only just occurred to him, and she looked back at him thoughtfully.

'That's an odd word for someone who's got everything,' she said. 'If I felt like that, I don't think I'd ever leave my ranch.'

'I've got a company to run,' said Matt, irritated and already beginning to regret having said as much as he had. 'I can't just give everything up.'

'Why not?' asked Flora practically. 'I mean, it's not as if you don't have plenty of money. You don't need any more.'

'You obviously don't understand how money works,' he said grouchily, and her face lit with a sudden smile that took his breath away.

'Funny,' she said, 'that's just what my bank manager says!' And then, when Matt said nothing, 'Go on.'

'Go on?' Matt made an enormous effort to shake off the strange feeling that had gripped him when Flora had smiled. 'What about?'

'Go on telling me about yourself.'

'Why do you want to know?'

'I'm interested,' said Flora. 'And I'd like to hear about the States—I'd love to go there one day.'

Matt paused while the waiter put their plates down with a flourish. 'What do you want to know?' he asked eventually.

'Oh, you know...' Flora waved her fork with an expansive gesture. 'Where do you go apart from Montana?

Where did you go on holiday when you were little? That kind of thing.'

'When I was a small boy, we used to spend the summer in Martha's Vineyard.' It was odd, Matt thought. He hadn't thought about those summers in years, but suddenly he could remember the smell of the ocean so clearly that if he closed his eyes he could almost swear that he could hear it. 'One of my first memories is walking along a beach between my parents. They were swinging me between them, and laughing.' He stopped, shaken by the clarity of the memory. 'My father used to take me sailing,' he went on slowly. He had forgotten that, too, until now.

Suddenly his gaze focused on Flora's warm blue eyes, and he shook himself back to the present. 'That's all a long time ago,' he said almost brusquely. 'I haven't been there for years.'

'So where do you go on holiday now?' she asked, and he shrugged.

'The Virgin Islands for sailing, Aspen for skiing, the ranch if I want some time to myself.'

'It sounds so glamorous,' said Flora enviously. 'We used to get dragged up to Scotland every year, all fighting in the back of the car.'

'You have brothers and sisters?'

'Two brothers. We used to spend our whole time squabbling, but we get on fine now.'

'I used to wish I had a brother or a sister,' said Matt. 'It didn't matter so much once I went to Harvard, but at school I always wanted a family. When my father died I inherited all the controlling shares in Elexx. I didn't have to do anything with them, of course, but I always knew I had this great responsibility waiting for me. My father had very high standards, and I had to live up to them. That isn't easy to do when you're eight.' He tried to shrug off the memory. 'After he died, I felt responsible for my mother as well as the company. A brother or a sister would have been someone to share that with.'

Poor little boy, thought Flora. 'So you *were* lonely?'

'I guess I was.' Matt suddenly realised that he was talking to Flora in a way that he had never talked to anyone before, and he frowned. Why was he telling *her* all this? 'Excuse me,' he said abruptly, getting out his mobile phone. 'I just want to check on the Tokyo market.'

Flora watched him from beneath her lashes as he made his call. She was sorry that he had suddenly clammed up, but she wasn't surprised. She guessed that he was a man who believed that sharing any kind of emotion made him somehow vulnerable.

He kept the conversation strictly impersonal for the rest of the meal, so obviously regretting having confided in her that Flora began to feel guilty for having asked him anything about himself at all.

It was as if, having opened up so briefly, Matt had retreated once more behind an impenetrable barrier. Anyone would think she wanted to prise his deepest darkest secrets out of him, Flora thought, collapsing tiredly onto the tube a few days later. She had only been making conversation, but Matt seemed to have viewed her with suspicion ever since. He had been even more demanding than usual, never letting up the pressure, and if his aim had been to make sure she didn't have a spare moment to ask him any more probing, intimate questions, like whether he liked watching movies or not, he had certainly succeeded! It would be a relief when he went back to New York for a short trip the next day.

That was what Flora told herself, but as soon as Matt had gone she found herself—well, *missing* him. Somehow the office seemed muted and colourless without him. Whenever the phone rang she found herself hoping that it would be his voice at the other end, even if it was only to issue yet another stream of orders, and

when he walked into the office three days later she was
ridiculously pleased to see him.

Matt had been glad of the chance to get away for a
while. Flora had become altogether too distracting a
presence in the office, and he had hoped that a few days
back in New York would remind him of his priorities.
The girl assigned to assist him there had been a model
of efficiency and discretion, but Matt had found himself
wondering at odd times what Flora was doing. He'd been
able to picture her with disconcerting accuracy. She had
only been working for him a few short weeks and already he felt as if he knew her. He knew the intent look
in her eyes as she typed, the animated expression as she
talked on the phone, the way her skirt swirled around
her legs when she walked across to the photocopier, the
irritating tune she hummed as she waited by the fax machine.

Irritably, Matt would push her image away. He had
flown back to London determined to keep her at arm's
length, but the first thing he saw when he walked into
the office was Flora standing there, smiling at him with
her blue eyes full of sunshine, and somehow he was
smiling back at her like a fool.

'I wasn't expecting you until tomorrow,' she was saying, and Matt managed to quash a quite irrational desire
to go over and kiss her—just in greeting, of course.

'Things have started moving at last on the French
merger,' he said gruffly. 'I spoke to Paris last night. The
deadline's next Wednesday, so we'll have to get moving.'

It was a frantic week. Flora was in the office by eight
in the morning, and often didn't leave until ten at night,
but there was something exhilarating about working under that kind of pressure. After that one smile, when she
could have sworn that he was glad to see her, Matt had
reverted to his usual disagreeable self, snarling down the
phone, erupting out of the office without warning with

unreasonable demands, or dropping huge piles of work on her desk without so much as a please or a thank you. And yet, when he was there, everything seemed sharper and clearer than it had done before, and the air crackled with invisible, invigorating energy.

At last it was done, and Flora was bitterly disappointed to find that after all her hard work Matt was going to take all the papers to Paris without her. 'There's nothing for you to do there,' was all he said. 'You may as well carry on with things in the office.'

It wasn't fair, Flora thought sulkily on the day of the signing. It was her deal as much as his! It was typical of Matt to drive her into the ground and then swan off to take all the credit and have all the fun without so much as a thank you! The office was empty without him, and echoed with anticlimax, and for the first time Flora went home on time, feeling more depressed than she could remember. It was tiredness, that was all. That was what she told herself, anyway.

When she went into the office the next day, there was a huge bunch of flowers lying on her desk. 'They're for you,' said Matt, appearing in the doorway.

'For me?' Flora gathered them up in delight. It was like picking up a meadow, and she breathed in the heady fragrance with a smile.

'It's to say thank you for all your hard work,' he said, trying to sound gruff. 'And sorry you didn't get to Paris.' He hesitated. 'I missed you,' he added, as if the words had been forced out of him, and Flora raised her head slowly from the bouquet.

'Did you?'

Matt swallowed at the sight of her standing in the sunlight with her arms full of flowers. 'We all did,' he said almost curtly, and turned abruptly back into his room.

Flora was left standing there, looking at his closed door in confusion. That was typical of Matt, too. He let her decide that he was thoroughly unpleasant, then took the wind out of her sails by giving her flowers. And now, just as she realised that she had been mistaken about him, he stomped off as if he resented having had to make the gesture at all.

But he had said that he had missed her. Flora looked down at the flowers and smiled.

She found a bucket of water and stood the flowers in it before knocking on Matt's door. He had his laptop computer open when she came in. 'I just wanted to thank you for the flowers,' she told him. 'They're beautiful.'

Matt, who had been staring blankly at the screen and wishing that he had somehow phrased things differently, glanced up. 'I'm glad you like them,' he said gruffly. 'We wouldn't have made that deadline if it hadn't been for you.' He got to his feet and moved round the desk towards her. 'I just want you to know that I appreciate all your hard work,' he said. 'I know I can be a difficult person to work for at times.'

Flora smiled. 'You're not difficult,' she teased. 'You're impossible!'

Matt looked back at her. 'I know,' he said, and then they both laughed.

Once they had started, it was impossible to stop smiling, until at the same time they realised that the spontaneous warmth had faded to be replaced by something strange and intangible and oddly unsettling. It held them there, their smiles almost uncertain, unable to move or to speak or to do anything but look at each other.

When the phone rang in Flora's office, they both started. 'I…er…I'd better get that,' said Flora, backing towards the door, half relieved at the interruption, half reluctant to go.

The memory of Matt's smile fizzed along her veins and she hugged it to her as she picked up the phone, but her pleasure blinked out when she discovered that it was Venezia Hobbs on the other end. There was a tiny pause when she told Matt who it was, and then he said curtly, 'Put her through.'

Well, what had she expected? That because he had given her flowers he would never talk to another woman? Flora found herself sighing, and promptly took herself to task. She had worked hard and Matt had shown that he appreciated it, as any decent boss would. It was ridiculous to think that their relationship had changed one jot as a result.

She was even able to tell herself she didn't care when Matt asked her to book a table for two for lunch that day. So what if he was taking Venezia out? In a few months she would be off on her travels, and she would be having much too good a time to wonder whether Matt was smiling at Venezia the way he had smiled at her. Flora pulled out the brochures she kept in the bottom drawer of her desk and leafed determinedly through them that lunch-time. She had to decide whether to fly straight to Australia, or do part of the journey overland through Southeast Asia, and she would much rather be doing that than sitting in some intimate restaurant with Matt Davenport...wouldn't she?

Matt, meanwhile, was not enjoying his lunch. He had asked Venezia out on an impulse. There had been a moment when Flora had stood there smiling at him when he had found himself wondering what it would be like to kiss her, and the realisation made him uneasy. It was just as well that Venezia had rung when she did. She was the kind of girl he felt comfortable with—happy to enjoy his wealth and wise enough to know that the slightest suggestion of emotional involvement would drive him away.

So why did he spend the whole lunch remembering how Flora had looked with her arms full of flowers and her eyes as warm and blue as a summer sky?

He was *not* going to let his PA distract him from his work, Matt decided firmly. He had a company to run and a billion-dollar deal to set up, and no woman was going to get in the way of that, no matter how blue her eyes.

Just to remind himself of how little he cared what Flora thought, Matt asked out a succession of girls over the next two weeks, careful to ensure that none of them expected any kind of enduring relationship.

Flora was soon fed up with making restaurant bookings for cosy lunches or candlelit dinners. Sometimes the girls came to meet Matt at the office. Like Venezia, they were all blonde, leggy and impossibly glamorous, and all had the most ridiculously contrived names.

It just went to show that her mother had been quite wrong when she had insisted that men were more interested in personality than in looks, Flora reflected, unreasonably depressed by Matt's taste in women. She smiled coolly at them all, though, and went back to planning her route to Australia. She had her own life to lead. If Matt liked mindless blondes, that was up to him.

It didn't stop her feeling huffy when Matt went out for lunch one Friday and didn't come back until five o'clock. And when he called her into his office and announced that he wanted to dictate some urgent letters, she exploded.

'It's quarter-past five!'

'So?' said Matt, without looking up from a letter he was reading.

Flora glared at him. 'This may surprise you, but I do have a life beyond this office! I realise you think I should be grateful for something to do on a Friday night, but it just so happens that I've got somewhere to go this evening!'

He looked up at that. 'Got a date?' he asked in a hard voice.

Flora toyed with the idea of pretending that she had, if only to show him that at least someone found her attractive, but in the end she decided against it. 'No,' she admitted a little sullenly. 'I'm just meeting a few friends at Covent Garden, and I said I'd be there by six.'

'It doesn't matter if you're a few minutes late, surely?' said Matt with an edge of impatience, and Flora's eyes flashed.

'I wouldn't have to be late if you gave me work in the morning instead of keeping everything for a rush at five o'clock,' she snapped. 'Everything is always "urgent" with you!'

'That's the nature of business at this level,' he said coldly. 'It's known as pressure.'

'What's pressurised about a four-hour lunch with your latest bimbo?' retorted Flora, enraged. 'I notice nothing was so urgent that you couldn't manage that! How come things are only urgent when *you're* ready to deal with them?'

'It may interest you to know that I was at lunch for less than an hour,' said Matt thinly. 'I went straight on to a meeting in the City and spent the rest of the afternoon there, as a result of which I'm at last able to send the details of a thirty-million-dollar deal to the New York office so that they can work on it. Of course, that was before I realised my secretary downed tools at five o'clock!'

Somewhat deflated by the knowledge that Matt hadn't in fact spent the afternoon with his girlfriend, Flora was still reluctant to back down. 'I haven't downed tools,' she said sulkily. 'I was just pointing out that I don't want to spend the entire evening in the office. If it really is important, then of course I'll stay.'

'No, no!' Matt held up his hands in mock horror. 'I wouldn't hear of it! What could possibly be important about thirty million dollars compared with your date?'

'It isn't a *date*,' said Flora in exasperation. 'I've told you, I'm just meeting some friends.' She flicked open her notebook and made to sit down. 'If you want to give me the most urgent stuff—'

'Certainly not!' he said with a martyred air, waving her away from the chair. 'I'm just your employer. You'll have to excuse me for getting ideas above my station. Far be it from me to keep you working when you could be out enjoying yourself!'

'Look, I've already said—' she began, but Matt had leapt to his feet and was ushering her sarcastically towards the door.

'Off you go,' he said, opening it with a mock chivalrous flourish. 'You have a good time! Don't worry about me or the future of Elexx. What's thirty million dollars, after all?'

Flora was so angry by that stage that she didn't even bother to answer. She was damned if she was going to beg Matt to let her stay and type his rotten letters for him! Instead she shrugged on her jacket, picked up her bag and thanked Matt with equal sarcasm for letting her leave on time before stalking out, only just resisting the temptation to slam the door behind her.

Matt wasn't nearly so restrained. He stomped back into his room and banged the door shut with such violence that a pile of files sitting on a nearby table shuddered in the blast, and the two at the top slid off and spilled their contents on the floor, which did nothing to improve Matt's temper.

Why couldn't Flora keep up with the filing? he wondered savagely as he shoved the papers back into the files, conveniently forgetting that he had told her not to put away anything in his room. He wasn't sure why he was so cross. The letters he had been planning to dictate weren't in fact so urgent that they couldn't wait until Monday, and he could e-mail any vital information to New York.

No, it was a matter of principle, he decided, slapping the files back onto the pile and only just preventing the whole lot sliding over again. Flora was his PA and that meant she should stay in the office until he said that she could go. Paige would never have dreamt of leaving while there was still work to be done, Matt remembered. She had never even mentioned her private life—unlike Flora, who obviously couldn't wait to drop everything and go out with her 'friends'.

Matt scowled as he sat down at his desk and switched on his computer screen. He had his own plans for later that evening, so why did the thought of Flora having a good time without him irritate like something stuck between his teeth? She would be at some bar right now, laughing with her friends, not giving a thought to him or to Elexx or to all the work she had left behind.

At that very moment Flora was in fact stuck on a crowded tube train which had stopped in a tunnel just before Piccadilly Circus. She was wedged between a City type in a grey suit and a gaggle of Spanish students, and had nothing to do but avoid making eye contact by looking at an advertisement for insurance. 'Cover yourself for the unexpected,' it urged her. Perhaps she should take out a policy against Matt Davenport ever being in a good mood for more than two minutes at a time.

The delay on the tube was so long that Flora was nearly half an hour late by the time she reached the wine bar where she had arranged to meet her friends. 'Matt Davenport been keeping your nose to the grindstone?' enquired Seb as she squeezed in beside him.

'Something like that,' said Flora, still breathless from running up the escalators. She and Seb had been getting on so much better since they had decided to split up, but she could never quite forget that as an ambitious reporter Seb was more interested in a story about Matt than in her.

Seb poured her a glass of wine from a carafe. 'Have you asked Davenport if he'll give me an interview yet?' he asked.

'No,' said Flora. They had this conversation every time she saw Seb now. 'Matt doesn't give interviews;

I've already told you that. You'll have to speak to the Media Relations Unit.'

'They're no use,' grumbled Seb. 'I need to speak to him himself. An interview with Matt Davenport would be a real scoop. I'm sure you could wangle it with him if you tried.'

To Flora's relief, her flatmate Jo leant across the table to interrupt them just then. 'Flora, we've just been talking about the ball.'

Jo worked for a charity which was organising the ball as a glittering event to raise funds, and she had conscripted as many friends as she could to make up a party. 'I need to find out the exact numbers of tickets we need,' she went on. 'Seb's taking Lorna, so that'll make eleven of us—unless you want another ticket?'

Flora turned to stare at Seb. 'Lorna?'

Seb smiled back at her with a trace of smugness as he spread his hands disarmingly. 'We *did* agree to go our separate ways…'

It was true. Still, Flora hadn't expected him to find a replacement for her quite that quickly. And Lorna! She had been angling for Seb for years!

Flora drank her wine defiantly. She couldn't help feeling a little piqued. It wasn't that she minded Seb going out with another girl, but her ego was distinctly bruised. It was bad enough having Matt's girlfriends rammed down her throat every day, without ex-boyfriends replacing her with indecent haste!

'It doesn't matter if you haven't got a partner,' said Seb condescendingly. 'We're all going as a group anyway.'

Flora lifted her chin at that. 'Who says I haven't got a partner?'

'You're not going to bring Jonathan, are you?' asked Jo with foreboding. She had suffered Jonathan before. A mother's dream, Jonathan was clean-cut, well mannered and extremely boring. Much to their amusement, and

Flora's despair, he was inexplicably devoted to her, in spite of all her attempts to discourage him.

'No,' said Flora, who had indeed been planning to ask Jonathan, just to save face.

'Who, then?'

Afterwards, Flora wondered what madness had seized her, but at the time all that mattered was wiping that smug look off Seb's face. 'Matt Davenport,' she said casually.

'*Matt Davenport* is taking you to the ball?'

She could tell that Seb thought she was bluffing, and couldn't resist the temptation to string him along a bit. She lowered her eyes coyly. 'I'd rather have kept it a secret, but Matt's so jealous at the idea of me going anywhere without him now,' she sighed.

There was a stunned silence. Obviously none of them could quite decide whether she was joking or not. 'But I thought he was going out with that model,' said Sarah after a moment.

Flora's eyes narrowed at the mention of Venezia. 'She's just a decoy,' she said airily. 'If the Press think he's involved with her, they won't hassle us.'

'You're having an affair with Matt Davenport?' said Jo incredulously. She still hadn't forgiven Matt for his comments about her precious pink skirt. 'When did this happen?'

'You remember all those nights I told you I was working late on the French deal?' Flora cast down her eyes demurely and allowed herself a reminiscent smile. She was beginning to enjoy herself. It served Matt right. Taking his name in vain wasn't much compared to all the times he had shouted at her! 'We weren't working at all,' she confessed. 'Nothing like that has ever happened to me before,' she went on brazenly. 'One minute we were standing close together, looking at the contract, and the next he was kissing me. He's so passionate and masterful, I just couldn't resist!'

The expressions around the table ranged from suspicion and disbelief to astonishment and envy. 'Why haven't you told us before?' asked Sarah.

'We didn't want anyone else to know about it,' said Flora, getting into her role. 'The secrecy was part of the excitement. But now Matt says he's madly in love with me, and he wants to be part of my life, so of course he wants to meet you all. I thought the ball would be a good opportunity,' she added casually.

Jo stared at her in sudden doubt. 'Flora, you're not really bringing Matt Davenport to the ball, are you?'

'Of course she's not,' scoffed Seb. 'She's having us on!'

That was the time for Flora to laugh and admit that she had just been joking, but Seb sounded so sure of himself that she didn't see why she should give him the satisfaction of being proved right. Besides, everyone would feel sorry for her then, thinking that she had just made up a partner because she was jealous of Lorna.

So, instead of doing the sensible thing and sharing the joke, Flora lifted her chin proudly and met Seb's sceptical gaze. 'Am I?' she said, blue eyes bright with challenge. 'Wait until the ball, Seb, and then see if I'm joking or not.'

CHAPTER FOUR

IT TOOK Flora nearly a week to pluck up the courage to ask Matt if he would take her to the ball. At first it seemed that all she could do was to carry on pretending until the last moment and then confess that she had indeed been joking, but the thought of Seb's face when she had to admit that she had been bluffing was almost more than she could bear.

After all, why *shouldn't* she ask Matt? He had said that he appreciated her hard work when he gave her the flowers, so he might be prepared to play along for her sake. It was worth asking him, anyway, she told herself. He had so many girlfriends, surely it couldn't make much difference to him if he pretended to take out one more? If he said no—and she had to face it, he probably would—she would just find another partner.

As she sat on the tube, Flora practised in her head what she would say to Matt. It always seemed easy then, but somehow the right opportunity to approach him never arose, or if it did her nerve failed her. By the time Wednesday came round, with only ten days until the ball, she was determined not to let another day go past without tackling him.

Taking a deep breath, Flora picked up a folder of carefully typed letters and knocked on Matt's door.

'Come!' he called in a brusque voice.

It didn't sound very encouraging. He didn't even look up as Flora laid the letters on his desk. 'You just need to sign these,' she said nervously.

'OK.'

No 'thank you', she noted dourly, but didn't say so.

She had been on her best behaviour for the last three days and she wasn't about to blow it now.

She cleared her throat. 'Er...have you got a minute?'

'I've got thirty seconds,' said Matt, without taking his eyes from the computer screen. 'Will that do?'

'Not really,' said Flora. 'When we ask if you've got a minute, what we really mean is: can you stop doing whatever you're doing and listen to me for as long as it takes?'

He did glance up at that. 'I may only be an American, but I do speak the same language,' he said, with an ironic look in the cool green eyes. 'I know perfectly well what you mean—which is why I told you I only had thirty seconds, all of which you have just wasted!'

'The thing is, I wanted to ask you a favour,' confessed Flora. 'I was hoping to get you in a good mood.'

'In that case, I suggest you come back later!'

'I've been doing that for days now,' she said glumly. 'You're never in a good mood!'

Matt sighed and turned his chair away from the computer so that he faced Flora across the desk. 'You're obviously not going to go away until you've had your say, so you'd better do it now before I really am in a bad mood!'

Having got this far, Flora was suddenly doubtful. 'Well, it's a bit difficult,' she said hesitatingly.

'Just get on with it, Flora!' barked Matt, and she sat down abruptly in the chair opposite him.

'Um...you remember I told you about Seb?' she began.

'No,' he said unhelpfully.

'Yes, you do,' Flora corrected him, annoyed at being balked so early in her story. 'He was my boyfriend, but we split up because I wanted to travel and he didn't.'

'The conversation isn't exactly engraved on my heart,' said Matt, resigned. 'But I do vaguely recall you telling me something of the kind.'

'We're still good friends,' she plunged on with relief. 'I mean, I wasn't upset when we broke up or anything. In fact, we've got on much better since we split.'

For some reason Matt didn't want to hear about how well Flora was getting on with her ex-boyfriend. 'What's it got to do with me?' he said, scowling.

'I'm coming to that,' said Flora. Now that she had started, she was beginning to get into her story. Maybe it wasn't going to be so bad, after all. 'Before we split up, we'd arranged to go to a ball with a group of friends. We all met up to discuss it the other evening, and it turns out that Seb is already going out with someone else and he's taking her to the ball as his partner.'

She paused expectantly, waiting for Matt to share her sense of pique, but he just sat there looking impatient.

'And?'

'And...well, it's not that I'm *jealous*,' Flora hastened to assure him, although it had to be said that Matt showed absolutely no signs of needing reassurance. 'It's just...I suppose I was a bit peeved that Seb had found another girlfriend so quickly.'

'Is there a point to all of this?' asked Matt acidly. Flora could say what she liked, but she sounded jealous to him, and he didn't see why he should have to sit and listen to her going on about some other guy.

'I'm trying to get to it.' Flora pleated her skirt, nervous now that she had to confess exactly what she had said. 'We were talking about the ball, and I could tell that everyone thought that I was jealous because of Lorna—that's his new girlfriend—so I thought I'd pretend that I had a partner too. It was just a joke at first but I—' She stopped and took a deep breath. 'I said that you were taking me,' she finished in a rush at last.

She had half thought that Matt would explode with rage, but instead he just raised a contemptuous eyebrow, which was *far* worse. 'Why would I do that?' he enquired, with a humiliating mixture of irony and incredulity.

'Because you're madly in love with me,' said Flora sullenly. She hadn't expected Matt to be pleased, but there was no need for him to make it quite so clear that the idea of taking her to a ball was beyond the bounds of all probability. She might not be one of his skinny blondes, but the suggestion that he might possibly find her attractive wasn't exactly *X-Files* material. 'I told them we were having a passionate affair,' she added, with a characteristically defiant tilt of her chin.

At least she had succeeded in capturing Matt's full attention. 'You said *what*?'

'I said we were having an affair.' Flora steeled herself to meet the angry green eyes. 'I know it was a bit of a cheek, but Seb was being so insufferable I just couldn't resist it. I just wondered—if you weren't doing anything a week on Saturday—if you'd come with me to the ball and convince Seb that we...well, you know...' She trailed off unhappily as the full enormity of what she was asking struck her for the first time.

'Let me get this right,' said Matt in disbelief. 'You want me to take you to a ball and spend the entire evening making love to you just to make your boyfriend jealous?' He was enraged. All those hours he had wasted trying not to think about Flora, and the only thing she wanted him for was to score points off another man!

'He's not my boyfriend any more,' said Flora, wishing that she had never started this.

'So why are you so desperate to make him jealous?'

'I'm not,' she said a little desperately, trying to make him understand. 'Look, Seb's a friend, and I'm very fond of him, but he always has to be *right* about everything.' Just like most other men she had known, she thought, but didn't say it. 'It just bugged me the way he immediately assumed that I was fibbing because I was jealous, and he's been telling everyone else that I'm just bluffing.'

Flora paused, but Matt's countenance was rigid and not in the least encouraging. Oh, well, she thought. 'I would just have loved to have seen Seb's face if I'd walked in with you and proved him wrong,' she went on after a moment. 'But it doesn't matter. Forget I ever mentioned it.'

She got to her feet and brushed down her skirt, reflecting that it might have been even more awkward if Matt had agreed. She couldn't imagine him getting on with any of her friends. 'I didn't think you'd come,' she confessed, 'but I thought it was worth a try. I might ask Tom to go with me instead.'

'Tom?' Matt practically bristled and she looked at him in surprise.

'You know—Tom Gorsky, in the Media Relations Unit.'

'I didn't know that *you* knew him,' said Matt, infuriated by Flora's insouciance. He could hardly believe that she would dare make up such a story, let alone ask him to take part in it, and now, when she ought to be feeling at the very least embarrassed and ashamed, she was airily suggesting dragging someone else into her stupid *joke*!

'We quite often have a chat,' said Flora, who was always ready to stop for a gossip and was by now on friendly terms with everyone from the senior management to the caretaker. 'He was saying just the other day that he'd like to get to know more English people.'

'And I suppose you're going to tell your friends that you're having a passionate affair with him too, are you?' Matt was illogically jealous at the very idea.

Flora laughed. 'No, I don't think they'd fall for that one again! Don't worry, I'll tell them all tonight that it was just a joke and that there is absolutely no chance of us ever having an affair, passionate or otherwise!'

'You'd better,' scowled Matt, but somehow he wasn't as relieved as he should have been.

Only Flora would dare to suggest anything quite so outrageous, he thought, torn between outrage, disbelief and a grudging admiration for her nerve. Had she really expected him to stand around making sheep's eyes at her while she tried to make her ex-boyfriend jealous? Matt had never played second best to anyone, and he wasn't about to start now!

He ran his eye frowningly down the list of e-mail messages awaiting his attention. She might at least have had the grace to seem disappointed, he thought, clicking crossly onto the first one. Anyone would think she would rather go to her stupid ball with Tom Gorsky! She had no right to sound so happy about the impossibility of their ever having an affair either.

It *was* impossible, of course, but *he* would decide that, not her!

Matt was grouchy for the rest of the day, and his temper was not improved that afternoon when Flora told him that his mother was on the line. Together, she and Flora were the most exasperating women he knew, and between the two of them it was a miracle he got any work done at all! Matt was in no mood to deal with his mother, but experience told him there was no point in trying to fob her off.

'Put her through,' he said wearily.

Flora was photocopying a confidential memo when Matt finally put down the phone. She didn't hear him come to his door at first and he was able to watch her as she stood by the machine, humming to herself, hips swaying in time to the tune she imagined she was producing, hands dancing through the air.

She even photocopied jauntily, thought Matt in something like despair.

'What's that phrase you use when you want someone to stop whatever they're doing and listen to you for as long as it takes?' he said, making Flora swing round in surprise.

'Have you got a minute?' she suggested, and he nodded.

'That's the one,' said Matt. He put his hands in his pockets and strode over to the window.

Below, the traffic surged round the square. The railed gardens in the middle were a green and tranquil oasis, and Matt could see two elderly ladies walking slowly together along the gravel paths.

Flora was deftly collecting the collated sheets, banging them together into neat piles and stapling them together with a loud snap. 'Did you *want* a minute?' she asked eventually, when Matt didn't say anything.

'Yes.' With a final look at the old ladies, Matt turned back from the window. He frowned at Flora's activity. 'Can you stop doing that and listen?'

'I've finished anyway.' She patted the pile into shape and looked expectantly at Matt. 'What is it?'

'When's that ball you were telling me about?'

'It's OK,' she said. 'I asked Tom at lunch-time, and he's going to come with me.'

'Cancel him,' said Matt, prowling over to her desk. 'I'm taking you.'

Flora looked at him in astonishment. 'I can't do that!'

'Why not?'

'I've already invited him,' she said, affronted by his peremptory command.

'Tell him I want to take you instead.'

'But I've just told him that you wouldn't!'

Matt made an exasperated noise. 'Well, you'll have to tell him that I've changed my mind. I thought you wanted me to go with you?'

'Maybe I've changed *my* mind,' said Flora frostily. 'It isn't that easy for a woman to ask a man out, you know, but Tom was so nice about it that I'm not sure I wouldn't rather go with him after all!'

'What about that boyfriend of yours? Wouldn't you like to see his face if you really did turn up with me?'

The thought of Seb's likely expression at the sight of her on Matt's arm would keep Flora happy for many months, she thought, but she couldn't help being suspicious.

'Why this sudden change of heart?' she asked as she carried the memos back to her desk. 'I got the impression you'd rather die than pretend to be in love with me.'

Matt's mouth turned down at the corners. 'I can't say I like the idea, but I need a favour from you, and in the circumstances I'm prepared to offer you a deal.'

'A deal?' Flora sat down behind her desk and looked at him in surprise. 'What kind of deal?'

Matt stopped pacing and turned to face her directly. 'I'll save your face at this ball, if you'll save mine with my mother,' he said.

Flora goggled at him. 'With your *mother*?'

'It's not really a question of saving face,' he corrected himself. 'More a case of keeping her quiet for a while.'

'But why? What's she done? She sounded so lovely on the phone.'

'Oh, yes, she's lovely,' said Matt in exasperation. 'Everyone loves my mother. She has only two aims in life. One is to flit around the world having a good time, and the other is to get me married so that she can be a grandmother.' He sighed. 'To hear her, you'd think that the only thing standing between her and certain death was the prospect of a grandchild, and this in spite of the fact that she's fitter and has more energy than most people half her age!'

Flora couldn't see what he was making such a fuss about. 'Every mother wants to be a grandmother,' she said placatingly.

'They don't work at it the way my mother does,' Matt said in a sour voice. 'She spends her time producing the kind of girls she thinks I ought to marry and ignoring anything I might have to say on the matter! Every time she calls me, it's to tell me about some other ''sweet'' girl she thinks I ought to meet. The latest is the daughter of some friend of hers. That was Mother on the phone just now, full of this Jo-Beth, who is apparently ideal for me in every respect. She even makes quilts, for God's sake!'

Swinging round, Matt caught the look of amusement on Flora's face. 'It's not funny!' he snapped, as she covered her smile with her hand. 'Now this Jo-Beth is coming to London—no doubt prodded by my dear mother,' he added bitterly. 'Mother wants me to meet her, take her out and generally look after her while she's in London. As if I didn't have a multi-national company to run!'

'Perhaps you could ask Venezia to help you out,' Flora suggested innocently. 'She was good at showing you London, wasn't she?'

Matt shot her a filthy look from the window. 'That won't be necessary. I told Mother she could relax because I'd fallen in love at last and was going to get married.'

A cold hand seemed to clutch at Flora's heart, and she swallowed hard, forcing herself not to mind. 'Congratulations,' she said bleakly. 'Who's the lucky girl?'

It would be one of those vapid blondes with the stupid names. Flora steeled herself.

'You,' said Matt.

There was a moment of utter silence while the office reeled around Flora. She shook her head to clear it. 'Who?'

'You,' he repeated impatiently. 'Why do you think I'm telling you all this?'

'But...but...' Flora stuttered. 'You don't want to marry me!'

'I don't want to marry anyone,' said Matt impatiently.

'That's the whole point! I just thought that if I said that I'd found someone that would get my mother off my back for a while.

'And don't look at me like that!' he swept on as Flora opened her mouth. 'I know I can deal with presidents and politicians and the toughest industrialists around the globe, so one woman in her sixties shouldn't present too much of a problem. I *know* I should be able to tell her firmly and clearly not to interfere in my life, but you don't know my mother. She's immune to any kind of logical reasoning, and argument just goes over her head.'

He brooded for a moment. 'At the time, it seemed a stroke of genius to call her bluff and simply pretend, but I should have known better. I thought she was going to be safely out of the way in Italy all summer, but now she says she's going to stop over in London on her way to Rome in order to meet you.'

Flora opened her mouth, couldn't think of a single appropriate comment, and shut it again. 'Why me?' she asked faintly at last.

'It was your idea,' Matt told her, and her jaw dropped. 'What do you mean?'

'You were the one who told your friends we were having an affair,' he pointed out.

'I didn't tell your mother we were going to get married!'

'You put the idea into my head,' he accused her. 'And when Mother asked me what my fiancée was called, yours was the first name I could think of.'

There was a tiny silence. Flora could feel a flush creeping up her cheeks, and she was having a ridiculous amount of difficulty meeting his eyes. 'She's never going to believe that you've fallen in love with your secretary,' she said at last, hating the constraint in her own voice.

'Your friends believed it,' said Matt, not sounding at all constrained.

'That's because they don't know you,' said Flora, resentment at his cool attitude sharpening her tone. 'Anyway, I'm not sure they *do* believe it.'

'They will when they've seen us together at the ball.'

'I don't know.' Unable to sit still, Flora got edgily to her feet. 'None of the guys would think to question how we felt, but it's a different matter trying to pull the wool over the eyes of your girlfriends! Jo and Sarah have known me for years. We'd never be able to fool them.'

Matt crossed the room until he was standing right in front of her, and Flora, with her back to the desk, found that she had nowhere to go. She could only look back at him, wide-eyed and wary, as he lifted his hand and very gently drifted his fingers from her cheek to her jaw and then down her throat. 'I think we could if we tried, don't you?' he said softly.

It was the merest graze of skin against skin, but Flora felt her face burning where he had touched her. Her heart was booming in her ears, and it took an enormous effort to jerk her head away and step sideways.

'Why don't you ask one of your girlfriends to help you out?' she said unevenly. 'Then you wouldn't have to bother trying to convince my friends. Your mother is much more likely to believe that you'd fallen in love with one of them.'

'Perhaps,' said Matt, 'but the fact is that I've already told her I'm in love with *you*, and I can hardly turn round and say that I've got my fiancée's name wrong, can I? Anyway,' he went on irritably, 'I couldn't make this kind of deal with any of the girls I know.'

'I don't see why not,' said Flora, relieved that he had moved away and was leaning against her desk. She took a deep breath and tried to calm her hammering heart.

Matt folded his arms. 'They might take me seriously, for a start—or get upset at the idea of being used.'

'Whereas my feelings don't matter!' she said tartly.

'I'm just a PA; I won't mind being used...is that what you mean?'

'No, it's not what I mean,' he said, nettled. 'But I know you won't get emotionally involved. You've made it very clear that your priority is to travel, and that you don't want to get married any more than I do. It just so happens that our interests coincide: you need me to back up this story you've told your friends, and I need you to support the story I've told my mother.' He paused. 'Wasn't it you who said that we were made for each other?'

'We're made for each other, darling.' Flora's words on the plane when they had first met seemed to reverberate now in the air between them.

She folded her arms defensively. 'I was joking.'

Matt sighed. 'Look, I'm only asking you to do what you wanted me to do for you.' He eyed her consideringly. 'I tell you what. I'll give you the price of a round-the-world ticket if you'll pretend to be engaged to me when my mother is here. That's not a bad exchange for a couple of hours over dinner.'

Flora looked at him in amazement. 'Are you serious?'

'It's a fair offer,' Matt countered haughtily.

Realising that he thought she was holding out for more money, Flora hastened to reassure him. 'I know it is—more than fair, in fact. I was just surprised that it should matter that much to you.'

'I know.' To her consternation, Matt gave a sudden rueful grin. 'You'd have to have met my mother to understand, but, believe me, it will be worth every penny to me if you can convince her that she doesn't need to push any more prospective brides my way for a while.'

'You'll have to tell her the truth some time,' said Flora, still breathless from the effect of his smile.

He shrugged. 'When Paige comes back and you go off travelling, I'll simply tell her it didn't work out. I might even be able to put off any of her future attempts at matchmaking by saying that I've never quite got over you.'

'That doesn't sound very likely!'

Matt straightened from the desk and looked at Flora's flushed face. 'I can think of more unlikely happenings,' he said slowly.

There was an airless pause. Flora wanted desperately to look away but couldn't. She could only stand there, held by that green gaze, while her heart began to slam painfully against her ribs and deep inside her something dangerous and disquieting uncurled.

'Well?' he asked softly.

'I...don't know.' Averting her face at last, Flora hugged her arms together and moved uneasily away.

'What's the problem? It's a straight swap. I'll pretend to be in love with you for an evening if you'll do the same for me.'

'It's not the same,' she said. 'You'd just have to be one of a crowd. I'd have to meet your mother face to face. I don't like the idea of lying to her, of pretending to be engaged when we're not.'

'I don't see the difference between that and pretending to be having a passionate affair and lying to your friends.'

'It seems different,' said Flora stubbornly. 'It would just be a joke as far as my friends are concerned, but I don't imagine your mother would think it was very funny. I wish I'd never thought of it now,' she confessed, turning abruptly to face him. 'It was a stupid idea.'

'Why?' Matt asked. 'It's not as if we'd be hurting anyone. If anything, it'll make my mother feel better to think that there's even a possibility that I might get married. All that would happen is that I would get some peace and you would be able to teach that boyfriend of yours a lesson. That's what you want, isn't it?'

Flora hesitated. 'Can I think about it?' she pleaded.

'Sure,' said Matt after a moment. There was no point in pushing her now. 'Can you let me know by Friday?'

His forbearance took Flora by surprise. Over the next two days, he made no reference to their conversation at all, and there was no question of him putting her under any pressure. Flora couldn't help thinking that it would have been easier if he had. She couldn't understand why she was dithering. She had wanted him to back her up at the ball and he had offered to do so. It would be a good joke and it would shut Seb up for a while, so why should it seem so different when it came to pretending to be in love for his mother?

Of course, it would be much easier at the ball, Flora told herself. All they would have to do was turn up together and dance a couple of times. But his mother would be watching them much more closely. On the other hand, she surely wouldn't expect a passionate display over the dinner table. Would it be so hard to spend a couple of hours batting her lashes at Matt and looking suitably infatuated?

She was just being stupid, Flora decided. Matt had been right: it was a straightforward deal. They would do each other a favour and then they would get back to being boss and PA. A round-the-world ticket was a round-the-world ticket, after all. And it *would* be fun to see Seb's face when she walked in with Matt...

It wasn't until they had finished work on Friday that Matt asked her if she had come to a decision. Flora had even begun to wonder if he had forgotten all about it. 'I'll do it,' she told him.

'Good,' said Matt briefly. 'When is this ball?'

'Next Saturday,' said Flora, thinking that he might have *tried* to sound a little more excited.

Matt was noting it in his diary. 'And my mother arrives the following Wednesday.'

'So,' she said awkwardly. 'What happens now?'

'I guess we'd better discuss exactly what we're going

to say,' said Matt. He glanced at his watch. 'Are you doing anything this evening?'

'I'll probably just meet the others at the pub.'

'If we're supposed to be having this passionate affair, they won't be surprised if you don't turn up, will they?' said Matt. 'Come on, I'll take you out to dinner and we can talk about how we're going to play it then.'

He headed towards the door, but Flora hung back. 'That's not really necessary, is it?'

'It is if we want to convince your friends and my mother that we really are lovers,' he said. 'I know you're a believer in just doing and saying the first thing that comes into your head,' he went on nastily, 'but I like to do things properly, and that means a bit of preparation. Now, get your things and let's go.'

Since he was already striding out of the office without giving her a chance to reply, Flora had little choice but to grab her bag and run after him. She could see that it was sensible to get their stories straight, but it was deflating to see the cold-blooded way Matt was approaching the idea of pretending to be in love with her. He didn't have to make it quite so obvious that he would have to put such a lot of work into it, did he?

He took her to a restaurant tucked away behind the King's Road. It was tiny, discreet and disconcertingly intimate, and Flora felt very self-conscious as she watched Matt scanning the wine list. It wasn't the kind of place you came for a business meeting. It was the kind of place you brought your lover—a place where you could hold hands over the table, or even exchange a kiss without anyone else seeing.

Not that Matt was likely to lean over and kiss her, Flora remembered with an inward sigh. He had probably chosen it precisely because no one he knew would be likely to see him with someone so unsuitable.

When the wine waiter had taken himself off, Flora judged that it was time to show Matt that she was in no

danger of misreading the intimate atmosphere of the restaurant. 'Venezia Hobbs has obviously done a good job
of showing you London,' she said in her bright, social
manner. 'You seem to know it better than I do. I must
have walked down King's Road hundreds of times without ever knowing this place was here.'

'London's full of places like this where you least expect them,' said Matt. 'It's one of the reasons I like it
here.'

'Don't you miss New York?'

Matt looked across at Flora's vivid face, at the bright
eyes and the wide mouth that always seemed on the
point of curling into a smile. 'Not right now,' he said.

Another awkward silence fell. It was his turn to think
of something to say, thought Flora bolshily, but Matt
seemed quite unconcerned by the lack of conversation,
and in the end, of course, it was she who broke it. 'What
shall I tell Tom Gorsky?' she asked. 'The last time I saw
him it was to ask him to the ball. It's going to seem
very rude if I tell him that I don't want him to come
after all.'

'I've already had a word with Tom,' said Matt. 'He
understands.'

'What do you mean, you've "had a word" with him?'
Flora looked at him indignantly. 'What if I'd said that I
wouldn't go ahead with the whole idea?'

'You didn't.'

'You didn't know that,' she accused him, and he
smiled.

'You don't get to run a multi-million-dollar company
without learning how to get people to do the things you
want them to do,' he said. 'I knew you wouldn't be able
to resist that round-the-world ticket, if nothing else.'

Flora's mouth set in a mutinous line. She would have
loved to have denied that the ticket had played any part
in her calculations, but she didn't think that she would

be able to carry it off convincingly. 'It's a lot to pay just for one dinner.'

'It'll be worth it if it keeps my mother off my back for a while,' said Matt humorously, and Flora eyed him in puzzlement.

'Why don't you just tell her that you don't believe in marriage?'

'Because it wouldn't be true.' That intriguing glint of humour vanished from the green eyes and he was suddenly serious. 'It's *because* I believe in it that I won't get married unless I'm sure I've found the woman I want to spend the rest of my life with. I'm not prepared to get married for the sake of it, only to get divorced a couple of years later if it doesn't work out.'

'But your mother would agree with you, wouldn't she?'

'Sure, but she's been pushing nice girls my way for the last ten years, and there hasn't been one I've wanted to give up everything for. I just end up feeling trapped when they start talking about commitment when we've hardly got past the first date.' Matt's smile was rather twisted. 'I'm thirty-eight now. I guess if I haven't found that special girl by now, I'm not likely to,' he added with an edge of self-mockery. 'I'm better off sticking to girls who know the score and aren't interested in any long-term relationship.' He glanced across at Flora. 'You seem surprised.'

Not for the first time, Flora found herself wishing those cool eyes weren't quite so keen. She shrugged, and concentrated on crumbling a roll between her fingers. 'I just didn't have you down as an all-or-nothing man, that's all.'

'Well, now you know.' Matt's expression was unreadable. 'What about you? Are you an ''all-or-nothing'' *girl*?'

Flora thought about it. 'In a different way,' she said slowly. 'Of course I'd like to get married and have children one day, but not until I've done all the things I want to do. I want to see the world first, to…oh, I don't know…to *live* a little before I settle down.'

'That's why you're the ideal person to help convince my mother,' said Matt after a moment. 'At least I know you won't get emotionally involved.'

Flora looked down at the roll in her hands and suddenly realised that she didn't want it. She dropped it onto the side plate. 'No,' she said in a flat voice. 'Of course not.'

CHAPTER FIVE

SHE *wouldn't* get involved, Flora told herself. Still, she wished she could sound as detached as Matt did as he suggested a possible outline of the story they would tell his mother and Flora's friends. Flora was horribly conscious that her own attempt to appear cool only made her sound strained and brittle, but how could she sound impersonal when she had to talk about how they might have fallen in love, how he might have proposed, when all the time she was intensely aware of him sitting across the table?

She couldn't keep her eyes off his mouth, off his hands, off the line of his jaw and the breadth of his shoulders. He was near enough to touch. She could lean over and curl her fingers around his, and she had to keep her feet tucked behind her chair to stop them sliding suggestively against his legs. She tried to concentrate on what he was saying, but talking about where Matt might have kissed her only made her wonder what it would have been like if he *had*. Would that cool, severe mouth have felt as exciting as it looked? Would his fingers have been warm around hers? Would she have leant against his hard body and felt his arms close around her?

Flora swallowed hard. She had to stop this! There was more than a hint of desperation in her effort to turn the conversation back into the safe, neutral ground of the office, but Matt was treating the discussion as if it were work anyway, so perhaps he wouldn't notice.

Matt was, in fact, grateful for the change of direction. It had seemed such a good idea to establish a story that they could both stick to if questioned about their sup-

posed affair, as they inevitably would be, but his attempt
to keep the discussion impersonal had foundered early
on. He was increasingly distracted by Flora, by the glow
of her skin in the candlelight and the gleam of her eyes
and the inviting curve of her mouth, by the memory of
how he had first seen her with her slender legs and her
hair tumbled over her face.

All in all, it was a relief when the meal ended and
they could stop avoiding each other's eyes. 'I'll drive
you home,' said Matt, overriding Flora's attempts to de-
mur, even though he knew it was probably a mistake.
But he could hardly take her out to dinner and then let
her get a bus home, he reasoned, unwilling to admit that,
having longed for the meal to be over, he was strangely
reluctant to say goodbye.

At least Flora had the directions to Wandsworth
Common to break the awkward silence in the car. Matt
could only nod and turn where she told him. Why hadn't
he just put her in a cab? Then he wouldn't have been
sitting there, feeling as tongue-tied as a teenager on a
first date.

By the time he pulled up outside the flat she shared
with two friends, Flora had managed to persuade herself
that she was being stupid. This was *Matt*, her boss. She
was just imagining the tension between them in the car.
Hadn't he made it clear that she was only with him tonight because he knew she wouldn't irritate him by em-
broiling him in all those embarrassing emotions that
went with his dread of getting involved? It was high time
she pulled herself together. The last thing she wanted
was for Matt to think for one moment that she found
him attractive. That would make working together much
too awkward.

'Well,' she said brightly as Matt switched off the engine. 'Thank you for dinner.'

'You know what you're going to say if anyone asks
about us?'

'As long as they don't ask anything too intimate.'

Matt turned in his seat to face her. 'Are they likely to?'

What did he think women talked about with their close friends? The state of the stock market? 'I don't know about your mother, but Jo and Sarah are bound to,' she said frankly.

'What sort of things are they going to want to know?'

'Oh, you know...' Flora fiddled with her bag, unable to meet his eyes. She wished she hadn't said anything now. It was all very well vowing to appear cool and unconcerned, but it wasn't that easy in the confines of a car with Matt's sharp gaze fixed on her face. 'Where we first kissed, what it was like, that kind of thing.'

'I see.' There was a pause. 'What will you say?' Matt asked at last, an odd note in his voice.

She moistened her lips. 'I don't know,' she said huskily. 'I'll make something up.'

'I've got a better idea,' said Matt, reaching out to smooth a stray hair behind her ear. 'I could kiss you now and then we'll both know what to say. Do you think that's a good idea?'

Think? How could she think when his fingers were sliding, warm and sure, down to her chin, and he was turning her face towards him? It was as if the merest graze of his fingers had sucked all the air from her lungs, leaving her breathless with a mixture of terror and anticipation. Her heart was slamming painfully against her ribs, and when she tried to speak all that came out was an inarticulate squeak.

Matt looked into her dark eyes. The squeak might have meant anything, but it hadn't *sounded* like a no, he decided, and allowed himself to lean slowly across and kiss her, as he had been thinking about kissing her all evening.

At the first touch of his mouth, Flora's lips parted in a tiny gasp that was part thrill, part shock at the electrifying jolt of sensation. This was what she had been thinking about all evening, and now it was happening and she was utterly lost. His mouth wasn't cool at all. It was warm, so warm, and exciting, and it felt so *right* to be kissing him back.

Helpless against a wash of sheer delight, Flora murmured with pleasure and her hands rose instinctively to slide around Matt's neck as she melted into him. She had forgotten that Matt was her boss, that she had determined to remain brisk and businesslike, that this was all just a pretence. All that mattered was the dangerous, unexpected delight of his kiss and the deep undercurrent of desire that was tugging her down into a torrent of sensation.

Dimly, Matt was aware that things were slipping out of control and he forced himself away from her. They faced each other across the handbrake, Flora dazed and uncomprehending and Matt's smile rather twisted. He hadn't meant to kiss her at all, but her mouth had been so inviting and her perfume had gone to his head, and suddenly she was there in his arms, responding with a sweetness that had thrown him off balance.

'I think we'll both be able to remember this part of the story at least,' he said unevenly, shocked by how much he wanted to go on kissing her.

Flora drew a ragged breath. She was trembling and the car still seemed to be spinning around her. *Story. Pretence. Business.* That was all the kiss had been about. Dredging up a few tattered shreds of pride, she made herself look back at Matt.

'I...I'd better go,' she croaked, determined not to give him the satisfaction of making an issue out of it. That wonderful kiss had obviously just been a detail to add a little realism to their storyline as far as Matt was concerned. Well, she could pretend that too, at least for as long as it took to get out of the car and up to the front door.

Matt nodded. 'I think you'd better go, too,' he said wryly.

He watched her as she walked up the path and let herself into the house before he shoved the car angrily into gear and drove back towards the centre of London, cursing himself for a fool under his breath.

Flora rubbed the steam from the bathroom mirror and gazed apprehensively at her reflection. Her stomach had been churning with nerves all day and now she felt empty and light-headed. Why had she ever embarked on this stupid pretence? She could have been looking forward to going to the ball as one of the crowd instead of having spent the entire week jittery and on edge at the prospect of spending the evening with Matt.

She had gone into the office on Monday determined to impress on Matt how little effect his kiss had had on her. If he thought she was going to be thrown by a casual peck like that, he had another think coming, Flora had told herself, ruthlessly suppressing memories of a weekend spent reliving every second of it. Unfortunately her cool dignity had been thrown away on Matt, who had simply carried on as if nothing had happened and had been as brusque and demanding as usual. Flora had been left torn between pique that he was able to put the kiss so completely out of his mind and relief that he didn't mention it.

She'd even begun to wonder whether he had forgotten the ball altogether, and it hadn't been until late on the Friday afternoon, when Matt had called her in to go through the diaries for the coming week, that she had plucked up the courage to remind him.

'OK, so that's the strategy meeting at three next Friday, and the charity reception in the evening,' said Matt at last. 'Is that it?'

'Yes.' Flora got to her feet. 'Er, you haven't forgotten about the ball tomorrow night, have you?'

Matt consulted his diary. 'Ball? Ah, yes, here it is. Who am I taking to that, again?'

He *had* forgotten! Flora looked at him in mingled outrage and dismay, but then he glanced up and she saw that he was smiling, and her heart did one of those absurd back-flips.

'Very funny,' she said wrathfully.

'Did you really think I'd forgotten?' he asked.

His smile was having the strangest effect on her. Flora felt hollow, as if her insides were dissolving with memories of how he had kissed her, and she wished that she were still sitting down. She clutched the desk diary to her chest for support as Matt checked the details of her address.

'Paul can take us to the ball, and then he can drop your bag off at the hotel,' he said, making a note to speak to the chauffeur.

Flora stiffened. 'What bag?'

'I thought you wanted to save face with your friends?' said Matt in surprise.

'I do.'

'They're not going to think much of our mutual passion if we go our separate ways at the end of the evening, are they?' he pointed out. 'If you want to save face, I suggest that you tell them you'll be sleeping with me instead of going back to your apartment.'

'*What?*' squeaked Flora.

'You needn't panic,' he said, with a sardonic lift of his eyebrow. 'The hotel suite has a second bedroom which my mother uses when she visits, so you can sleep there, in case you're worried that I might have designs on your virtue. And all your friends can imagine us spending the night making mad, passionate love.'

The colour had rushed up into Flora's cheeks as the idea of Matt making love to her presented itself with disastrous clarity. It should have been reassuring that he had been so open about not having any intention of sleeping with her, but somehow it had only made her more nervous than ever.

He would be here any minute. Every time the doorbell went, her heart stopped, but first it had been Jo's boy-friend arriving, and then Sarah's. Next time it would be Matt, and she had better be ready.

Flora leant towards the mirror to put on her lipstick just as the door buzzed. Her heart lurched into her throat so suddenly that her hand jerked, smearing lipstick all over her cheek. Heart hammering, she searched franti-cally for a tissue to wipe it off, while along the corridor she could hear Sarah opening the door. Even though she was expecting it, the sound of Matt's deep American voice made her freeze and her chest tightened in panic.

Her hand was shaking so much that she was left with a decidedly wavery line at her next attempt to put on her lipstick, but it was too late to do anything about it. Flora wiped her palms on her dress and forced herself to take a deep breath, before jerking open the bathroom door and walking straight down the corridor and into the sitting room before she had time to change her mind.

The first—the only—person she saw was Matt, sitting on the lumpy sofa, and she stopped dead. He looked devastating. The formal dinner jacket with a crisp white shirt and bow-tie threw his severe dark features and pale eyes into striking relief, and as he got to his feet Flora was so overwhelmed by the sight of him suddenly *there* that she forgot to breathe.

Dimly she was aware of Jo saying something, but she didn't even notice the others. She was conscious only of Matt, of his height, of the hard solidity of his body, of the smile that seemed to reach inside her and squeeze her heart.

'Flora...' Matt's voice sounded as if it was coming from somewhere outside him. After the last few weeks of being annoyed by the way Flora's image kept dis-tracting him at the most inappropriate moments, he was still totally unprepared for the way she looked. He had grown accustomed to the demure, rather dull clothes she had worn in the office since his scathing comments about her outfit on the plane. He was used to the way she pulled her hair sensibly away from her face, unlike the first time he had seen her when the wind had tangled it into a haphazard mess.

He had never seen her like this before, her eyes huge and dark and blue, her hair falling in a tumble of gold and honey to her shoulders, vibrant in a shimmering dress that revealed the warmth of her skin and the fullness of her breasts and the heart-shaking line of her throat.

'Hello,' Flora managed to croak.

Jo and Sarah were watching her with interest and fond envy, but she didn't even see them. Matt was holding out his hand, and with dream-like inevitability, Flora walked over and took it, let him pull her into the security of his body. It seemed the most natural thing in the world to lift her face invitingly, but Matt didn't dare kiss her in case he couldn't stop. His fingers tightened convulsively around hers, but, instead of kissing her lips the way he wanted to, he lifted her other hand and pressed his mouth into her palm.

'You look beautiful,' he said, without taking his eyes from her face.

Flora's bones melted at the warmth of his voice and she practically collapsed onto the sofa behind her. Her palm burned with the imprint of his lips. With an effort, her eyes focused on Sarah, standing behind Matt and sticking up her thumbs in an exaggerated gesture of approval, and she awoke abruptly from the trance-like state that had gripped her since she had walked in and seen Matt waiting for her.

'I—I'm sorry I'm late,' she said huskily.

Matt sat down beside her, close enough for their

thighs to touch. 'It doesn't matter,' he said. 'Your friends have been telling me *all* about you!'

'Don't look at me!' said Jo quickly. '*I* didn't tell Matt about the time you passed out in Bratissani's!'

And with that they were all off, competing with each other to remember the most embarrassing stories about Flora. Flora wanted the sofa to open up and swallow her. God knows what Matt would think of her now! But when she risked a glance at him, he was laughing. It didn't seem to have taken him any time to get on the best of terms with her friends, and Flora, who had worried in case he was as rude to them as he was to her, was conscious of an obscure sense of resentment. He never bothered to be that charming to *her*! Even Jo had forgiven him for his comments about her beloved pink skirt and was treating him like an old friend.

A fixed smile on her face, Flora bore with it all as best she could, but she was excruciatingly conscious of Matt beside her. He was sitting back, looking completely relaxed and at home, as if he spent his whole life in messy flats like this one. When Flora thought of the expensive, exclusive places he could be at this moment, and the glamorous people he could be with, she cringed with embarrassment, although Matt himself looked as if there was nowhere else he would rather be, and no other company he would rather have.

Flora was the one who felt awkward and out of place. She sat tensely on the edge of the sofa, gripping her glass as if her life depended on it. Matt's hand rested with casual possession against her bare back, tracing absentminded patterns with his fingers. Flora could feel them searing into her skin. If she stood up, she was sure that everyone would be able to see them tattooed onto her back.

Matt had provided a couple of bottles of champagne, and suggested taking the whole party to the ball in the limousine that was waiting outside—an offer that was enthusiastically accepted. 'You know, we all thought Flora was pulling our leg when she said you were coming to the ball,' Jo told him.

'Oh?' said Matt, pretending surprise. 'Why was that?'

'Well, she's kept you pretty quiet up to now.'

He couldn't resist smoothing the honey-brown hair behind Flora's ear. 'We just wanted to keep things to ourselves for a while, didn't we?'

Flora's cheek tingled where his fingers had brushed against it. She tried to speak, but the most she could manage was an inarticulate noise, and in the end she just had to nod.

Jo and Sarah regarded her with affectionate amusement. 'We've never seen Flora in love like this before!' Sarah told Matt. 'She even tidied the sitting room for you, and now she can't even talk.... It must be serious!'

Flora squirmed on the sofa, her face afire. If this terrible evening ever ended, she would kill her friends! She could feel Matt watching her profile.

'I hope so,' he said softly.

As if pulled by some invisible force, Flora's head turned to face him. He was smiling, and the green eyes were warmer than she had ever seen them before. They held hers for a timeless moment while the chatter and the laughter faded around them and left them marooned on the sofa, where nothing existed but the feel of his fingertips smoothing tantalisingly over her back and the sound of her heart booming in her ears.

And then Matt looked away to join in the conversation and Flora, shaken and disorientated, tried to pull herself together. She could see Sarah and Jo casting her puzzled looks, and knew they were wondering why, with a man like Matt Davenport sliding his hand possessively up and down her back, she wasn't over the moon. But how could she be the life and soul of the party when Matt's thigh rested so close to hers, and all she wanted was for the others to disappear and leave them alone so that she could turn to him and run her hand over the muscles in his leg, and kiss her way along his jaw to the pulse that beat so invitingly below his ear?

The image was so clear and precise that the breath stuck painfully in Flora's throat, and she gulped at her champagne in an effort to dispel the temptation. Matt was acting the part he had agreed, she reminded herself fiercely. He was her boss, not her lover, and she had better not forget it.

Seb's expression when he saw her holding Matt's hand was one that Flora would always treasure. A mixture of stupefaction, disbelief and chagrin, it made every embarrassment she had endured worthwhile. They had arranged to meet up with the rest of the party at the table, and Seb was standing talking to his new girlfriend when someone obviously pointed out Flora and Matt's approach and he spun round incredulously.

Flora was cock-a-hoop as they took their seats around the table. 'You were brilliant!' she whispered to Matt. 'Did you see his face?' Seb was vanquished, and now that Matt wasn't actually touching her, she could relax, and she was on sparkling form over dinner.

Matt watched her as she laughed and gesticulated, and wondered with a sickening twist of jealousy if this was all an elaborate charade to make Seb jealous, in spite of her glib assurances that it was just a matter of pride. Why else would she be so concerned about convincing her former boyfriend of her supposed affair? He eyed Flora moodily. The dessert had been cleared away while the band struck up, and she was leaning her elbows on the table, her face vivid as she argued light-heartedly with Jo's boyfriend about some movie.

Was she still in love with Seb? Was that what this whole evening had been about?

Abruptly, Matt pushed back his chair and reached for

her hand. 'If you want to convince Seb that you're besotted with me, we'd better dance,' he said.

He felt better when he had her to himself on the dance floor. It was already crowded, which gave him a good excuse to pull her into his arms, just as he'd been thinking about doing throughout that interminable dinner.

Flora was tense at first, holding herself stiffly away from him. It had been so much easier when they were eating, without the touch of his fingers to distract her. That had been her opportunity to remind herself just what Matt was doing there. They had made a deal; he was keeping his side of it, and when his mother arrived she would keep hers. And after that she would go back to being his secretary until Paige was ready to resume work, and then she would go off and see the world without him, just as she had planned for so long.

'I know you won't get emotionally involved.' Wasn't that what Matt had said to her? The last thing he wanted was for her to fall in love with him—not that she had any intention of doing *that*! That really would be a disaster. Oh, no, thought Flora, she wouldn't do anything so silly. If she knew what was good for her, she'd tell him she didn't want to dance any more and run away from the overwhelming temptation to throw caution to the winds and lean against him.

It was just that his chest looked so solid and inviting. It was just that the lights were dim and the music was slow. It was just that his hand was warm against her bare back, and if she relaxed—just a little—it might pull her closer still. Seb might still be suspicious, and be looking to see whether they were dancing like lovers. And her legs *were* feeling rather wobbly and in need of some support...

With a tiny sigh, Flora closed her eyes and gave in.

Matt felt her relax into him until her face rested against his collar and her breath feathered his throat, and, without thinking, he tightened his arms around her. His hand smoothed rhythmically up and down her spine. She was warm and pliant and irresistible. Resting his cheek against her hair, Matt felt its softness, breathed in her perfume, gathered her closer still, and felt Flora meld herself into him until her lips were just touching his throat.

He swallowed. This was a bad idea, the cold, rational part of his brain told him. A *very* bad idea. He didn't want to get involved with anyone at the moment, did he? Messy emotions made him uncomfortable, and it would all end in tears. When she wasn't being infuriating, Flora was a nice girl, and—more importantly—a good secretary. She was much more efficient than she looked, and at least she didn't burst into tears or threaten nervous breakdowns like the others he had tried to replace Paige with.

And right now, the unwelcome voice went on, he needed an assistant more than an affair. This European deal was vital to the future expansion of Elexx, and the last thing he wanted was to have to find a new PA at this stage. Wasn't the company he had worked so hard to build into a global force worth more than one woman, however desirable she might seem?

Of course it was. So stop holding her like you never want to let her go, said the ruthless voice inside him, and take her back to the table *right now*!

Matt knew that was just what he should do. And he *would* do it…in a minute. It was just that she felt so soft and warm in his arms, and the fragrance of her skin was making it hard to concentrate, and, when it came down to it, he was only a man, for God's sake!

'Let's go,' he said roughly in Flora's ear.

Afterwards, Flora could remember nothing of how they had left the ballroom. She supposed that they must have made their excuses and said goodbye, but she was conscious only of Matt's hand holding hers very tightly as he pulled her from the room. He had dismissed his limousine earlier, so they took a taxi back to his hotel. She remembered the taxi's yellow light, the ticking sound of its engine, the smell of its seats. She remembered how the streetlights and passing headlights threw Matt's face into relief, remembered too how cold and lost her hand felt when he released it. She clutched at the strap, convinced that if she let go an irresistible force would send her rocketing across the cab and that she would clamp onto Matt like an iron filing drawn to a magnet.

As they'd waited for a taxi to appear, the night air had cleared Matt's head enough for him to be appalled at what he was doing. Hadn't he just decided that he was going to keep his relationship with Flora purely professional? That meant letting go of her hand, for a start. He wouldn't touch her in the taxi, and when they got to his hotel he would take her up to his suite, show her the spare bedroom, and say goodnight.

Easy.

They walked through the lobby carefully apart, and waited for the lift in agonising silence. When it came, they stepped in, still without touching, and watched the floor numbers light up as they rose effortlessly upwards. The air between them twanged with a tension that was almost audible. Flora could feel it vibrating through her, tingling along her nerves and making her heart thud so slowly, painfully and erratically that it was a struggle to breathe.

She had been so sure that Matt wanted her when he dragged her from the ballroom, but since then he had made no move to touch her. Perhaps he didn't want her, after all. Perhaps he had just been bored. Oh, God, please make him want me, one part of Flora prayed as her body thumped with desire, while another, more sensible part shrieked frantic reminders about not getting involved and keeping her mind on the job.

At last they were standing outside the suite. Matt

glanced down at Flora, trembling with a mixture of fear and anticipation beside him, and then away. *No*! he told himself and concentrated on swiping the keycard through the door. Inside, the living area was lit only by a couple of table lamps, and Flora stepped gratefully into the shadows, terrified that Matt had seen the longing in her face.

Matt closed the door with unnecessary care and turned to see her, pale and luminous in the lamplight. This was the moment for him to show her the spare room.

'Flora,' he said instead, and reached for her.

The breath clogged in Flora's throat as his hands closed at her waist and he drew her slowly, very slowly, towards him. 'Flora,' he said again, his voice ragged with desire.

Flora could feel herself booming with anticipation, and she lifted her hands instinctively to spread them over his chest, closing her mind to the sensible urgings to step back and out of danger. Tomorrow she might regret this, but tonight…tonight she would take whatever Matt had to offer. She didn't care what happened in the future if only he would kiss her now.

Matt cupped her face between hands that were not quite steady, and when he bent his head Flora closed her eyes in exquisite relief.

And then, just as his lips were about to touch hers, a warm, cheerful voice called out, 'Matt, is that you?' and the next instant the overhead lights snapped on as a woman appeared through a door on the other side of the suite.

Matt's hands had frozen around Flora's face. He found himself looking down into her eyes, huge and shocked and a dark, dark blue in the overhead glare, and it was his turn to close his eyes briefly as his hands dropped to his sides with a suppressed groan.

'Mother,' he said with terrible restraint. And then, 'How did you get in here?'

'The hotel let me in, of course, dear. You know I always stay here when I'm in London, and you'd told them I was coming next week, so they weren't at all surprised to see me.'

Nell Davenport advanced, beaming, across the suite. From what Matt had told her, Flora had imagined a ruthless society matron, terrifyingly well turned out and adept at pushing aside anyone who stood in her way. Nell wasn't at all like that. She was certainly expensively dressed, but she was small and plump, with beautiful silvery hair and a warm smile.

'And don't say you weren't expecting me, Matt,' she was saying to her son, who towered over her, 'because you must have known that I'd want to come and meet Flora as soon as I could.'

She lifted her face expectantly, and Matt, who could cheerfully have strangled her, sighed and kissed her cheek. 'And you must be Flora,' she went on, turning to where Flora stood, still dizzy with the shock of being wrenched away from the certainty of Matt's kiss. Managing a nod and a weak smile, she found herself enveloped in a warm, scented hug. 'You're not at all as I imagined you,' Nell confessed, 'but I am so *thrilled* about you and Matt, I just can't tell you!'

'Mother!' Matt pulled himself together with an effort. 'You're not supposed to be here until Wednesday,' he said, unable to keep the accusing note from his voice.

'I know, dear, but I was having lunch with Leonie Greenberg yesterday—or was it today? I get so confused with time change!—and telling her how excited I was about you getting married at last, and she said she didn't know how I could wait to meet Flora, and then, of course, I realised that I *couldn't* wait, so I went straight home and packed a suitcase and got on a plane...and here I am!' she finished triumphantly.

'But what about your trip to Italy?' said Matt with foreboding.

'I'll go straight on from here on Thursday, just as I planned,' Nell told him. 'It means I'll have four days with you instead of just an evening!' She beamed at them both, and then, seeing their appalled expressions, looked startled. 'Is there a problem?'

A muscle was twitching in Matt's cheek. This was typical of his mother, he thought savagely, raging inwardly at her timing. Why couldn't she have waited until the date they had agreed? Even a day later would have meant that he and Flora would have been alone tonight. He could have been kissing her right now, and they would have had a whole night ahead of them to break every resolution he had made.

'It's very inconvenient,' he said tightly.

'Oh, nonsense!' said his mother, brushing that aside. 'How could it possibly be inconvenient when you live in a hotel suite with an empty room? Or are you going to tell me that Flora was going to sleep there?'

At the sound of her name, Flora roused herself to make an effort at last. She moistened lips that were dry with frustration. 'I...er...perhaps I'd better go home,' she said huskily. 'You'll want to be alone with Matt.'

'No, I don't,' said Nell frankly, eyes beginning to twinkle. 'Matt'll just be grumpy and disagreeable, especially if he thinks I've driven you away! Anyway, it's you I've come to see. There's no need for you to move out of Matt's room just because I'm here,' she went on, giving Flora's hand a reassuring pat. 'I'm not at all old-fashioned that way. We'll all stay here together, and that way, we'll have a chance to get to know each other properly, won't we?'

Flora, unable to think of a single thing to say, could only smile feebly and cast a helpless look at Matt, whose attempt to remonstrate with his mother was waved aside by Nell.

'Why are we standing around like this?' she said

gaily. 'We need to celebrate! Matt, dear, why don't you ask them to bring up a bottle of champagne?'

'Because it's one in the morning, Mother,' said Matt through set teeth. Flora was looking shattered by her first encounter with his mother, and he didn't blame her. 'You may not be tired, but Flora is.'

'Oh, dear, and I was so looking forward to a good chat!'

Her idea of a 'good chat' would be to interrogate Flora at length about her life, her engagement and no doubt their wedding plans, Matt thought grimly. 'You can chat in the morning,' he told her dryly, taking Flora's arm in a reassuring grasp. 'Right now, Flora is going to bed.'

Flora was intensely grateful to Matt for taking charge. Nell kissed her goodnight reluctantly, and promised that they would get to know each properly in the morning, although, in Flora's disordered state of mind, the promise sounded more like a threat.

Her relief at escaping from Nell's determination to celebrate their false engagement lasted only until Matt showed her into his bedroom, which led off the far side of the suite. This wasn't how she had hoped to see his room, Flora thought bitterly. If Nell hadn't appeared just then, she was sure that they would have ended up in here. She had seen it in Matt's face when he reached for her, and she knew that she hadn't wanted to resist.

But now the magic of that moment was broken and they were back in the bleak reality of pretence. Matt indicated her bag, which she had packed earlier and which the limousine had brought on to the hotel while they were at the ball. His expression was so cool and remote, his manner so distant that Flora was seized by sudden doubt. What if she had imagined that look on his face?

There was an awkward silence. 'I'm sorry about this,' said Matt in a constrained voice after a moment. 'I didn't plan for things to work out this way.'

'It's not your fault,' said Flora, equally stiff.

She was standing by the door, looking oddly vulnerable. Matt longed to take her in his arms, but he was suddenly afraid that she would think that he was taking advantage of her. He *had* been going to take advantage of her, he realised with a twinge of guilt. She was his employee. What if she had felt that she had little choice in the matter?

'I'll sleep in the chair,' he said abruptly.

Thrown by his aloof manner, Flora was determined to show him that she was just as unconcerned by the prospect of spending the night together. And if he wanted to pretend that he hadn't been about to kiss her out there, well, two could play at that game!

'There's no need for that,' she said coolly, nodding at the huge bed that dominated the room. 'I'm sure it's big enough for both of us, and I know you'll be the perfect gentleman.' She gave a brittle smile. 'Sharing a bed won't bother me if it doesn't bother you.'

Matt was quite sure that it *would* bother him, but he could hardly say so when Flora was making it so clear that she would prefer to ignore the fact that the evening would have ended very differently if only his damned mother hadn't appeared just then.

'Fine,' he said, with something of a snap. 'I'll leave you to get ready, then.' He headed towards the door before he changed his mind. 'The bathroom's over there. I'd better try and persuade my mother to go to bed too.'

He went out, closing the door behind him, and Flora was left to wash her face and brush her teeth and persuade herself that there was absolutely no reason why two adults shouldn't share a huge bed without falling on each other in a fit of passion. Matt would lie on one side and she would lie on the other, and that would be that. It would be fine.

CHAPTER SIX

OF COURSE, it wasn't fine. It wasn't fine at all. In fact, it was one of the worst nights Flora had ever spent.

Matt didn't come back for what seemed like hours. Obviously waiting until he was sure she'd be asleep in case she threw herself at him the way she had at the ball, Flora thought, burning with humiliation. The longer she lay there, the more she was convinced that she had misinterpreted Matt's actions. He had been keeping his part of the bargain by pretending to be in love with her, and she had repaid him by clinging to his neck, snuggling into him and all but begging him to kiss her!

It was just as well Nell had arrived when she did, Flora decided as she tossed and turned in a vain attempt to get comfortable. At least it had given her a chance to remember that being lovers *was* just a pretence. Tomorrow, she would make it clear to Matt that she hadn't forgotten, however it had appeared tonight.

Flora wished she could sleep, but her heart jumped at every sound, and, when the door finally did open, she froze. Lying rigid under the duvet, she heard Matt moving quietly around the bathroom, the click as he switched off the light before he came out. The sound of the duvet being pulled back was like a pistol-shot in the strained silence.

The mattress dipped slightly, then Matt was in bed beside her. If she rolled over, she would be able to touch him. Flora squeezed her eyes shut against the image and willed herself to sleep, but how could she sleep when she tensed every time he stirred, or felt the duvet shift as he settled himself more comfortably? Straining her ears, she listened to him breathing. In, out. In, out. Deep and even. Clearly Matt wasn't the slightest bit bothered at the prospect of sharing a bed with her! He was just going to lie there and relax until he fell asleep, Flora realised with incredulous resentment.

Matt had never felt less relaxed in his life. He was staring up at the ceiling, concentrating savagely on counting to a hundred and then backwards to one, and then in French, and then to whatever figure it took to stop him thinking about Flora lying only inches away. Part of him was glad that she was asleep, but it would have been nice to have known that he wasn't the only one lying there with his body raging in frustration. It was all right for her, but he'd be lucky if he got any sleep at all.

When he woke the next morning, Flora was still sound asleep. She lay sprawled over the bed, her face burrowed in a pillow and her hair tumbled over her shoulders. Matt watched her for a while with a frown that was both baffled and resentful. What was it about her that unsettled him so much? She was just an ordinary girl, not particularly beautiful, not particularly clever. The only remarkable thing about her was the way he seemed to lose control over things when she was around.

Easing himself out of bed, he made his way to the kitchenette and moodily drank a cup of strong coffee before pouring a second cup for Flora, refilling his own and taking them to the bedroom. Flora had rolled over and was clutching his pillow now, Matt noted sourly. It hadn't taken her long to move in on his side of the bed.

He put the coffee down beside her and went to pull the curtains. Sunlight poured into the room, striping Flora's face. She stirred and mumbled something into the pillow before rolling over onto her back and blinking herself awake. The first thing she saw was Matt, looking down at her with an indecipherable expression.

'I've brought you some coffee,' he said.

The coolness in his voice brought Flora fully awake with a jerk, and she hoisted herself up onto the pillows, pushing her hair away from her face. 'Thank you,' she said awkwardly. She would have preferred a cup of tea, but it didn't seem tactful to say so.

'We need to talk,' said Matt, sitting down on the edge of the bed.

Oh, God, what if she had talked in her sleep? What if she had snuggled against him in the night? Was that why she had woken on his side of the bed? He might be going to ask her to keep her hands to herself in future... 'Yes?' she said a little breathlessly.

'I spent some time last night trying to persuade my mother to cut her visit short,' he said, rubbing his neck wearily at the memory. 'I told her we were too busy to entertain her, I told her we just wanted to be alone, I tried everything I could think of, but none of it made any difference. Mother has decided that she's staying until Thursday and that's that.'

Matt picked up a coffee and handed it to her. 'It means, of course, that we've now found ourselves in the awkward position of sharing this room for the next few days,' he went on carefully. 'I didn't expect you to have to do more than come out to dinner one night, but now the situation's rather different. I'm afraid I'm going to have to ask you to pretend for longer than we originally agreed.' He drank his own coffee morosely. 'I guess it wasn't such a good idea after all.'

'It's worked, hasn't it?' said Flora, who, remembering the resolve she had made last night, was bent on proving to Matt that she had no more forgotten their agreement than he had. 'I'm not complaining. Thanks to you, I didn't look a fool in front of my friends and Seb was certainly convinced. That was all that mattered to me.'

So her performance last night had been aimed at her ex, Matt realised, obscurely resentful. Leaning against him, resting her head on his shoulder, letting him think that she wanted *him* and all along she had obviously been keeping an eye on Seb's reaction over his shoulder!

He scowled down into his cup. It should have been a relief to discover that Flora showed no sign of misinterpreting the way he had held her last night, but instead Matt was conscious of an odd sense of dissatisfaction. Now he would have to make it clear that he was approaching a potentially awkward situation in an equally businesslike spirit.

'I'll pay you, of course,' he said coolly. 'Shall we say five hundred pounds for each extra night you have to stay here?'

Flora's jaw dropped. 'You must want to keep your mother quiet!' she said.

'I do,' he said briefly. 'Will you do it, or do you want more money?'

'No, that sounds fine,' she said hastily, trying to get excited at the prospect of earning so much money in such a short time. By Thursday, she would have two thousand pounds *and* the cost of a ticket! With what she was earning as his PA there would be nothing to stop her heading off as soon as Paige was ready to come back to work, so why wasn't she more thrilled at the prospect?

Perhaps she had a hangover.

'I expect you to be convincing for that kind of money,' Matt warned as he got to his feet.

Flora sent him a clear look over the rim of her coffee cup. If he could be that cool about the whole embarrassing business, so could she! 'I will be.'

She reminded herself of her promise as she dressed. When she had packed her bag, she hadn't expected to be on show to Matt's mother, so she had just brought her old jeans, a white T-shirt and her much-loved fawn cardigan, which was shabby and shapeless but indescribably comforting. Flora eyed her reflection a little dubiously. Heaven only knew what Nell would think! She must have been expecting her son to have chosen someone with at least a veneer of sophistication.

Still, there was nothing she could do about it now. She would just have to act the part of an adoring fiancée that little bit harder. And she would. Matt had done as much for her, and now she was on the verge of all her dreams coming true. She was incredibly lucky, Flora reminded herself. Her debts would be cleared and she would be able to go wherever she wanted as soon as Paige came back. All she had to do was pretend to be in love with Matt for a week. That couldn't be so hard, could it? It ought to be the easiest money she had ever earned. As long as she didn't make a fool of herself, as she had so nearly done last night, it would be easy.

Having talked herself into a buoyant mood, Flora went to find Matt and his mother. Nell was by the window, enthusing about the view of Hyde Park, but, when she saw Matt's face change suddenly, she turned.

'Flora, dear! How pretty you look! Doesn't she look lovely, Matt?'

Matt didn't answer immediately. He was knocked off balance by the sight of Flora, her hair still damp from the shower, her skin glowing and her eyes very blue. It had been shock enough to see her in that dress last night, but now she was in her casual clothes he felt as if he was seeing the real Flora for the first time. She was vibrant, alert, shimmering with health and spirit, and he thought she looked beautiful, but he wished she would put her hair up and go and change into the dull, secretarial outfit she wore to the office. It would make it so much easier to remember who she was and what she was doing there.

He cleared his throat. 'You look very nice,' he said.

'Very nice?' Nell looked at him in surprise. 'Is that all you can say?' She glanced from one to the other and Flora realised that for all her bubbling warmth and charm Matt's mother had uncomfortably shrewd eyes. 'He's not much of a lover, is he?'

Flora looked at Matt and mentally took a deep breath. Now was the time to earn her money. 'He is when it matters,' she said, and smiled as she went over to him, sliding an arm around his waist and leaning against him so that she could look playfully up into his face. 'Aren't you, darling?'

As if it had a will of its own, Matt's arm closed around her. The natural thing would be to kiss her, he told himself. It need only be a brief kiss, just to convince his mother. 'As long as you think so,' he said, succumbing to heady temptation.

Flora's lips parted as his mouth came down on hers. Remembering how helplessly she had abandoned herself when he had kissed her in the car, she tried to brace herself against the electric excitement, but it was no good. At the first touch of his lips, her bones dissolved and she was swamped by a breathless wave of sheer delight at the warmth and persuasiveness of his kiss.

Her fingers clutched at his shirt in a sort of desperation. She mustn't let herself go! She was *acting*, that was all. She couldn't afford to let Matt guess how his slightest touch set the world reeling around her. He mustn't know how desperately she wanted to kiss him back, how much she had wanted him to kiss her like this last night, how, deep down, she wanted him to kiss her because *he* wanted to, and not because his mother was watching.

Just a brief kiss, an inner voice nagged at Matt. *That's long enough. Let her go.*

Reluctantly, he raised his head, and deliberately avoided Flora's eyes. Instead he encountered his mother's interested gaze. 'Why, Matt,' she said with some amusement, 'you look quite peculiar! Anyone would think you'd never kissed her before!'

A faint flush crept along Matt's cheekbones and he

dropped his arm, which had been holding Flora close against him. 'Don't be ridiculous, Mother! I told you I'd fallen in love—or did you think I was making it up?' he added, with what Flora thought was unnecessary daring.

'Well, it *did* seem very sudden,' Nell admitted. 'You'd never even mentioned Flora, and the next thing I know you're calling me to say that you're getting married! Naturally I *wondered*.'

Flora forced a smile. 'It all happened very quickly. Sometimes I wonder if it's really happened myself!' Her legs were still wobbling alarmingly, and she could have done with Matt's arm back to support her. She hoped Matt didn't realise how completely she fell to pieces when he kissed her. 'And I was so dopey last night that I'm not surprised you wondered what exactly was going on.'

'That was my fault for not letting you know that I was coming,' said Nell, obviously remembering how they had expected to have the suite to themselves when they came back last night.

Flora congratulated herself on allaying one doubt anyway. If they weren't what they said they were, why would Matt have brought her back to the hotel? 'I think your visit calls for a celebration,' she said, getting determinedly into her part. 'Shall we get them to send us up a champagne breakfast?'

'Oh, my dear!' Nell clapped her hands in delight. 'A girl after my own heart!'

She drew Flora down onto the sofa beside her while Matt ordered breakfast. 'Now, I want to know *all* about it!' she warned. 'Was it love at first sight?'

Flora glanced at Matt, who was putting down the phone. He was looking irritated, the corners of his mouth turning down in exasperation at his mother's question. He would have to do better than that if he wanted to convince her!

'Definitely not,' Flora told Nell, and leant forward

with a confiding air. 'To tell you the truth, I thought he was awful when I first met him!'

Nell seemed amused. 'That's always a good sign,' she said, and looked speculatively at her son, who had sat on the arm of the sofa next to Flora. 'What about you, Matt? When did you fall in love with Flora?'

There was a tiny silence while her question seemed to reverberate in the air. For an unnerving moment, Matt felt as if he had stumbled upon a chasm and was teetering terrifyingly on the edge, but he pushed the feeling aside. Lifting his hand, he stroked Flora's hair.

'I don't know,' he said with an unreadable expression. 'I just looked across at her one day and knew that she was the only woman I would ever want.'

A wave of colour swept up Flora's cheeks. He sounded so convincing, she thought wistfully, and then chided herself. She was meant to be remembering how lucky she was to be able to travel, not wondering what it would be like if all this were for real.

To her relief, the subject was dropped when breakfast arrived, and quietly forgotten in the business of sitting at the table, passing croissants and opening the champagne. 'When is the wedding?' Nell asked, shaking open her napkin.

'We're not sure yet,' said Flora, just as Matt said,

'We're not announcing anything formally until this deal has gone through.'

They both stopped and looked at each other in consternation. 'Why not?' said Nell.

'What do you mean?' asked Matt after a moment.

'You're both single, you're both in love,' his mother pointed out with just the slightest edge of sarcasm. 'What possible reason could there be not to let anyone know about your engagement?'

There was another awkward pause before Flora rushed into speech. 'We haven't told my parents yet,' she said, earning herself a look of gratitude from Matt. 'They're away...on a cruise,' she improvised, with a mental apology to her mother, who suffered terribly from seasickness and refused to set foot on so much as a ferry. 'They won't be back for another three months.'

'I see,' said Nell. There was a ghost of a smile about her mouth, and Flora had a nasty suspicion that Matt's mother hadn't believed a word they had said so far. They must both sound much too vague and uncertain. Perhaps she had better try and be a little more specific.

'I know exactly what the wedding's going to be like, though,' she told Nell. 'We're going to get married from my parents' home in Yorkshire,' she said. 'Just family and friends. There's a beautiful medieval church in the village, so we can walk from the house and we don't need to worry about grand cars. I thought it would be nice to keep everything private and very simple,' she went on, warming to her story. 'We could have a small marquee in the garden and decorate it with cow-parsley, so it was like being in a summer meadow.'

'*Cow-parsley?*' said Matt before he could stop himself.

'You remember I told you about it, darling,' said Flora with a dagger look. 'It's that wild flower that looks like lace and froths along the hedgerows in early summer.'

'Oh, yes,' muttered Matt, who had no idea what she was talking about. 'We don't get that much of it in Manhattan.'

'It sounds charming,' said Nell.

Flora couldn't help thinking that her impromptu ideas *did* sound rather appealing. It was just a pity they would never be realised—or at least not with Matt as the groom. She couldn't imagine him walking her back from the church along the village street, or being polite to her aunts amidst the cow-parsley, and suddenly she felt vaguely depressed.

'I do hope you're going to make Matt have a proper

holiday afterwards, Flora,' Nell was continuing. 'He needs a complete break from that company of his!'

Since his company's money was paying for the champagne she was drinking, let alone ensuring her a life of wealth and comfort, Matt thought his mother could well have left Elexx out of it. He drank his coffee, feeling disgruntled. Why did women get so excited about weddings? Flora had obviously been planning hers for years. He wondered whom she imagined waiting for her at the top of the aisle in her medieval church. Not him, obviously.

Now Flora was talking about honeymoons. He had to hand it to her: she was being very convincing. It was clear that his mother adored her already. He ought to be pleased, Matt remembered. Wasn't this just what he had wanted? Nell wouldn't waste any more time finding him suitable brides now that she had met Flora, and he would easily be able to persuade her that he was broken-hearted once Flora had gone.

Once Flora had gone... A feeling that Matt preferred not to identify twisted sharply inside him. He fought it down and tried to concentrate on the conversation instead.

'We're going for at least three months,' Flora was saying a little indistinctly as she licked croissant crumbs from her fingers. 'And if Matt makes so much as a phone call to the office in that time, I'll sue for divorce!'

'You didn't tell me about that condition,' Matt said, deciding that it was high time he curbed Flora's imagination before his mother began to suspect something.

But Flora, buoyed up by the champagne, was well away. 'I'm telling you now,' she said pertly. 'We're going to places where the phones don't work and there's no such thing as e-mail,' she informed Nell with an extravagant gesture. 'We're going to sit on top of sand dunes and watch the sun set. We're going to swim in warm lagoons and lie under coconut palms and at night we're going to sleep under ceiling fans and listen to the sounds of the tropics.'

Daringly, she rested her hand on Matt's. 'Aren't we, darling?' she said with a provocative play of her eyelashes, but, if she had hoped to disconcert him, she was disappointed. Instead of recoiling in horror at the idea, as she had half expected, he turned his hand beneath hers so that their palms were touching and linked their fingers together.

'If that's what you want,' he said, looking straight into her eyes. Flora wasn't the only one who could act around here!

'Well!' said Nell humorously. 'It must be love!'

Matt didn't take his eyes from Flora's face. He lifted their entwined hands and kissed Flora's. 'It is,' he said softly.

The expression in the green eyes held Flora in thrall. Her whole body seemed to be humming with awareness, and deep inside her a strange sensation fluttered into life, spreading outwards until it shivered just beneath her skin.

Neither of them noticed the arrested look on Nell's face. She watched them gaze at each other in silence, and drank her champagne, suddenly thoughtful. 'If it's love, why haven't you bought Flora a ring?' she asked, when Matt wrenched his eyes away at last and released Flora's hand.

Matt cursed inwardly. He should have thought about a ring. 'I've already told you that we're working on an extremely important deal at the moment, Mother,' he said repressively. 'We don't have time for anything else.'

'It wouldn't take you more than half an hour to buy a ring!'

'Flora doesn't mind waiting until we're less busy, do you?' Beginning to feel hunted, Matt appealed to Flora, who achieved a martyred little sigh.

'Not if you don't think you can spare the time,' she said wistfully, and he shot her a warning look which she ignored. 'Matt works much too hard at the moment,' she confided to Nell instead. 'But I don't really mind because I know that will all change once we're married. He won't be able to spend all those hours in the office when we have a family.'

Nell paused with her coffee cup halfway to her lips. 'You're planning a family?'

'We want at least four children,' Flora told her and, caught unawares, Matt choked into his coffee beside her. Serve him right, he should have bought her a ring, she thought flippantly, and patted him on the back with exaggerated concern. 'Don't we, darling?' she added naughtily.

'I can't wait,' he managed between coughs.

Nell was watching them in amusement as she drank her coffee. 'To think of Matt as a father at last!' she said. 'Why, I remember when he was a little boy—'

'Uh-oh!' Hurriedly swallowing the rest of his coffee, Matt pushed back his chair and got to his feet. 'If you're starting on little boy stories, I think I'll go and make some calls.'

'Matt! You're not going to the office on a Sunday!' Nell and Flora regarded him in equal dismay.

'I may as well. It's only five minutes away, and I'm sure you'll get on much better without me,' he said dryly, bending to kiss his mother's cheek to forestall any argument. 'You two finish the champagne and I'll come back to take you out to lunch.'

He came back to Flora and twined his fingers in her hair so that he could tilt her head back gently. 'Don't believe everything Mother tells you, will you?' he said, and then—just because his mother was watching, he re-assured himself—he stooped to kiss her lightly on the lips as any lover would do.

Flora was better prepared this time, but even so the

brief caress was enough to send a slow, treacherous shiver of response down her spine. Could he hear her heart beating? Did he know what he did to her whenever he touched her? Flora closed her eyes and prayed that he didn't.

'I'd better go,' said Matt, surprised to find that his voice could sound so even when inside he was reeling from the sweetness of her lips and the beguiling scent of her skin.

'Goodbye,' she said huskily.

His hand slid reluctantly down the silky hair and he hesitated a moment before turning abruptly and striding out of the suite without another word.

Still dazzled by that one brief kiss, Flora stared after him until the door shut with a decisive click. Her throat felt tight and she had a horrible feeling that she might be about to cry. When she looked back at Nell, she found that she was being watched with a very odd expression.

She swallowed. 'Is something the matter?'

'Quite the contrary,' said Nell slowly. 'I'm sorry, was I staring? I was just thinking how different you are to what I expected when Matt told me he was getting married, and yet now that I've met you I can see that you're perfect for him.'

Flora busied herself pouring more coffee for them both. Perfect for him? The only thing Matt found perfect about her was the fact that she wouldn't embarrass him by getting emotionally involved. 'Tell me about Matt as a little boy,' she said, suddenly desperate to change the subject. 'What was he like?'

'Stubborn!' said Nell, laughing and throwing up her hands. 'Once Matt made up his mind to do something, nothing—but *nothing*!—was going to stop him. Just like his father, of course.'

She sighed, remembering. 'He was always a serious little boy. I often wonder if he would have been less reserved if his father hadn't died when he did. I think he felt as if he had to be responsible for me.' She shook her head sadly and then looked at Flora, her gaze very clear and direct. 'I know I drive Matt crazy sometimes, but he puts up with whatever I do. He'd never admit it, but he does everything for me. He gets a bit crabby sometimes but I know that he loves me underneath it all.

'He's so like his father it hurts me to look at him sometimes,' Nell went on. 'Scott was a very private man too. Everyone thought *he* was cold, but I knew better.' A reminiscent smile touched her lips. 'It took Scott a long time to settle down, but once he'd fallen in love with me he never looked at another woman. I wasn't even forty when he died, you know. I've had other offers of marriage since then, but I could never love another man the way I loved Scott.'

Flora was feeling terrible about deceiving Matt's mother. Poor Nell, who had lost the man she loved so early. No wonder she clung to the hope that Matt would start a family she could share in.

Reaching across the table, she squeezed Nell's hand. 'You must have been so lonely,' she said.

Nell's smile was rather shaky, but she pressed her lips together and put her other hand over Flora's to pat it almost fiercely. 'It's all a long time ago now. I just wanted to make sure that you understood what Matt is really like. He has this image of a hard, ruthless businessman but he's not like that at all. The only person he's really ruthless with is himself. He's a one-woman man, and he needs someone to love him the same way.'

Flora looked across at Nell. 'I know,' she said quietly, and the strange thing was that she did.

By the time Matt returned, Flora and Nell were firm friends. They were both still sitting at the table where he had left them. The breakfast debris had been cleared away, but they had evidently ordered more coffee, for a large pot was placed in the middle of the table. Flora was resting her elbows on the table, her hands cradled around her cup and her hair, now dry, pushed casually behind her ears. She was laughing at something Nell had said and, seeing the two of them together, Matt felt his heart stir strangely.

'Back already, dear?' exclaimed Nell in delight, and Flora, turning her head quickly, felt the air driven from her lungs in a great whoosh of breath as she saw Matt in the doorway, tall and lean and darkly formidable.

'It *is* twelve-thirty,' Matt pointed out. 'I can see you've missed me!'

His sarcasm went over his mother's head. 'We've been having a lovely time,' she told him. 'We've just been talking about how to get you to spend less time in the office.'

Matt came over to the table. He ought to greet Flora, but he didn't dare kiss her again in case he really did lose control this time. He compromised by sliding his hand beneath her hair and resting it at the nape of her neck where he could caress her warm skin with his fingers. 'And what did you decide?' he asked.

Flora, burningly conscious of his tantalising fingers and the instinctive response that shuddered down her spine, set her cup back in its saucer rather unsteadily. 'Nell thought you'd want to spend time with your children,' she said, quite proud of how natural she sounded. 'But I was hoping that it would be me you'd want to spend time with.'

'It'll always be you,' said Matt, his hand tightening a fraction. 'Why do you think I don't want to marry you until this European deal has gone through? If you're not in the office, I'll never get any work done.'

'It didn't seem to stop you this morning,' said Flora, not quite able to keep the tart edge from her voice. She had enjoyed Nell's company, but it hadn't stopped her missing Matt. Only because it had been a strain to maintain the pretence on her own, she added hastily to her-

wonderful. Perhaps this complicated pretence they had embarked on would work out after all.

Watching him, Flora sensed that Matt was more relaxed than she had ever seen him before, and she was suddenly intensely happy just to be with him. The situation they were in might be artificial and temporary and doomed to end in tears—probably hers—but at that moment it was enough to be sitting in the sun beside him.

And, since they did have an agreement, she had a perfect excuse to touch him after all. Succumbing to temptation, Flora reached out and let her fingers drift possessively over his forearm and down to his wrist before twining her fingers around his with a smile.

Matt made no effort to pull his hand away as she had been half afraid that he might have done. 'What is it?' he said, turning from Nell.

'Nothing,' said Flora. 'I'm just happy.'

Matt's chest felt oddly tight as he looked down at her and instinctively he returned her clasp. 'Are you?' he asked, and his voice held a rough, almost urgent undertone.

She looked straight into his face and wondered how she could ever have thought his eyes were cold. They were warm and green, and in them lurked an expression that she couldn't identify but which sent the blood thrilling along her veins.

'Yes,' she said simply.

Her strangely exhilarated mood lasted throughout lunch. Flora was on scintillating form, teasing Matt— with much encouragement from Nell—and letting her imagination take flight as she pretended increasingly elaborate plans for their future. Matt listened to her, appalled at the very idea of the life she was gaily imagining for his mother's benefit. She was doing it deliberately, that much was obvious, and he didn't know whether to be cross at the way she was pushing Nell's credulity to the limits with her outrageous stories, or amused at her daring.

When Flora started on the house parties they would have, Matt decided that it was time to put a stop to her. He put a restraining hand on Flora's shoulder. 'Where are you staying in Italy, Mother?' he asked, interrupting her firmly.

Nell was in the middle of telling them about her trip when, to Flora's dismay, an eye-catching figure rose from a party on the far side of the terrace and came over towards them. Venezia, of course. What was *she* doing here?

Matt hadn't seen her yet. Flora touched his hand warningly and he glanced at her and then in the direction of her nod. His heart sank as he recognised Venezia.

He had met the model soon after he had arrived in London, and had admired her beauty and glamour. She had an astute business brain too, which he respected, but, although he had been careful not to give her any grounds for thinking that their relationship might progress beyond the purely social, on the last couple of occasions he had seen her Venezia had definitely been hinting that she was looking for some kind of commitment from him. Matt had recoiled at the very idea. He had no intention of getting emotionally involved with any woman, no matter how beautiful and intelligent.

Remembering his reaction, Matt's mind flickered to Flora, who was watching Venezia's approach with a combative expression on her face. *Any* woman?

Any woman, the ruthless voice inside his head confirmed firmly. Flora was here to convince his mother to leave him alone, and he could do without Venezia waltzing in and complicating matters.

'Don't mention the engagement,' he muttered out of the side of his mouth as he rose to greet Venezia, who had arrived at the table with her leggy, catwalk stride. Flora half expected her to pout and do a twirl for them.

'Matt!' said Venezia in her husky drawl. *So* affected when you came from Maidenhead, Flora thought vengefully, as the other girl presented her cheek for Matt to kiss with sublime confidence. Flora longed for him to ignore it, but of course he didn't. 'Why didn't you tell me you were going to be here today? I haven't seen you for ages! We could have come together. I would have dropped out of Ricky's party if I'd known.'

'We only decided at the last minute,' said Matt, avoiding his mother's eye. Venezia was looking expectantly at the fourth chair, and he had little choice but to pull it out for her. 'Sit down.'

'Thanks.' Venezia's sultry trademark smile was for him alone, and Flora's eyes narrowed dangerously.

Until Venezia had appeared, she had been perfectly content in her jeans, but now she felt lumpy and frumpish. Venezia was wearing jeans too, but somehow wearing them with style on her impossibly thin, leggy figure. No plain T-shirt for her, either. She had on some kind of gauzy top which left little to the imagination and which only a model could carry off. Flora eyed her with deepening resentment. Nobody had the right to look that good in clothes. It was unfair to the rest of womankind, who had to wear clothes they could do more than sit around in.

'I don't think you've met my mother, have you?' Matt was saying with a certain quiet desperation. He could sense Flora bristling beside him, and Nell looked none too welcoming either.

'Your mother?' Venezia turned her huge stare on Nell with sudden interest. 'No! How are you?'

'I'm fine,' said Nell, who hadn't approved of the proprietorial way Venezia had greeted her son. Flora, who had never heard her less than warm and bubbly, almost cheered at the frostiness in her voice.

'And you know Flora,' Matt went on.

Venezia cast an uninterested glance across the table,

a faint frown between her perfect brows. She was plainly not a girl who wasted much time on other women. 'I don't think...'

'At the office,' Flora said helpfully, with an overbright smile that made Matt nervous. 'I'm Matt's temporary PA.'

'Oh, yes.' It was obvious that Venezia couldn't imagine why Matt had even bothered to introduce her. She turned back to him and laid a caressing hand on his arm. 'I was hoping to see you when I got back from the shoot in Morocco,' she murmured, and Flora didn't even stop to think.

She took Matt's other hand. 'Darling, do tell Veronica our news!' she said with another brilliant smile, and had the satisfaction of seeing Venezia's huge eyes narrow, although whether at her endearment or the deliberate misuse of her name it was hard to tell.

'It's Venezia,' she said very distinctly. 'What news is this? Have you signed that contract that was taking up so much of your time?'

'Oh, it's much more exciting than that!' said Flora, leaning winsomely against Matt's shoulders and fluttering her lashes in a truly nauseating fashion. 'I'm not going to be temporary very much longer, am I, Matt? We're getting married next year, so I'll have a much more permanent position in his life—although of course Matt doesn't want me to work after the wedding,' she added with a simper that set Matt's teeth on edge.

'You're getting *married*?' Venezia was unflatteringly incredulous. She looked at him as if waiting to be told that it was all a lie. *'Matt?'*

A muscle was jumping angrily in Matt's jaw, and the look he cast at Flora promised signal vengeance, but, with his mother an interested and amused spectator, he could hardly deny it. 'We're not announcing anything publicly yet,' he said through set teeth.

'Oh, but you don't mind an old friend like Veronica—

sorry, *Venezia*—knowing, do you, darling?' cried Flora, ignoring the unmistakable message in his eyes and leaning defiantly across him to speak to Venezia. 'I do hope you'll come to the wedding,' she said, sugar-sweet, and was delighted to see that Venezia was looking distinctly cross. 'It was so kind of you to show Matt around London when he first arrived.'

Venezia's face tightened and she took her hand from Matt's. 'Is this true?' she asked him, as if they were alone, and then, lowering her voice, 'I thought you didn't want to get involved in a long-term relationship?'

Matt was furious at having been put in such a position by Flora. 'I've changed my mind,' he said curtly. What else *could* he say?

'I see,' said Venezia with a brittle smile. 'Well, congratulations. No, don't get up,' she added as she got to her feet a lot less languidly than she had sat down. 'I just came over to say hello, but I'd better get back to my party.'

Flora watched her stalk petulantly back to her table and could barely restrain a whoop of triumph. Matt was obviously livid, but she didn't care. He could hardly expect her to have sat there calmly watching while Venezia drooled all over him like that, could he? Chin lifted at an even more defiant angle than usual, she met Matt's eyes bravely.

There was a dangerous pause. Matt was longing to tell Flora exactly what he thought of her, but he couldn't say anything with his mother sitting there, and frustration tightened his jaw.

'Would you like anything else?' he asked through his teeth.

Nell opened her mouth to suggest that they leave, but Flora had no intention of scuttling off and leaving the field to Venezia, who was busy telling everyone at her table about the terrible mistake Matt was about to make, judging by the heads turning in their direction and the covert whispering that was going on.

'I'd love a pudding,' she said brightly.

It was nearly an hour later before Matt was able to drag her away, by which time he was seething with suppressed temper. 'Mother, you must be tired,' he said with careful control as they walked out to the car. 'Why don't I take you back to the hotel and you can have a rest while Flora and I go and pick up her things from her apartment?'

But Nell hadn't missed the jangling tension between the two of them, or the fleeting glance of appeal Flora had sent her. 'You know I never get jet lag, Matt,' she said, with what he considered downright obstructiveness. 'I'm not in the least bit tired.'

'Why don't you come with us, Nell?' suggested Flora gratefully. 'I just need to get some clothes for next week, but you could see the flat and meet Jo and Sarah.'

'I'd love to,' said Nell, earning herself a dazzling smile from Flora and a tight-lipped look from her son.

So Matt had to drive the two of them all the way to Wandsworth Common. He then had to wait while Flora dithered around packing a bag, and was forced to be pleasant to her friends, who were eyeing him with undisguised speculation. His mother, of course, soon had them charmed and, before he could refuse, was graciously accepting Sarah's offer to make tea. That was another hour and a half wasted, and then Flora nearly blew everything when Jo asked her if they should start looking for another tenant.

'You're not to let my room!' whispered Flora in a panic.

Jo looked at the suitcase Flora had packed. 'Aren't you moving in with Matt?'

'No…that is, not permanently.' Flora glanced at Nell, but fortunately Matt's mother was engrossed in conversation with Sarah and couldn't hear. If she hadn't been there Flora could have told Jo the truth, but she couldn't risk even giving her friends a hint with Matt listening to her every word. 'I mean, it might not work out,' she said rather desperately when Jo raised her brows in surprise.

Jo looked from Flora to Matt and then back again. 'I think it will,' she said.

Much she knew, Matt thought savagely. In the end, he didn't get Flora on her own until they went to bed. Flora and Nell had stuck together in frustratingly female solidarity all evening, but even his mother couldn't think of an excuse to spend the entire night with them. Matt took Flora by the wrist and practically dragged her into his room, slamming the door shut behind him.

'You can't hide behind my mother any longer,' he told her furiously. 'So perhaps you'd like to explain what the hell you thought you were doing today? I *told* you not to mention our engagement to Venezia, but did you listen? No! It was "Darling, do tell Venezia our news" before she'd had a chance to open her mouth!'

'I was only acting in character,' said Flora, rubbing her wrist resentfully. 'No self-respecting girl would sit there meekly while another woman manhandled her fiancé the way Venezia did!'

'Manhandling? All she did was touch my hand!'

'No, she didn't *just touch* your hand. She sat there stroking it and looking at you with those great big eyes of hers so that we all got the message that she was ready to drag you off to bed at the first opportunity,' Flora retorted, beginning to get as angry as Matt now. 'Your mother would never have believed that we were engaged if I'd just sat and smiled nicely! It's not as if you made any attempt to shake her off.'

Matt had sat down on the edge of the bed and was taking off his shoes and socks with a sort of suppressed fury. 'Why couldn't you have been satisfied with looking sulky or something? Now the whole world knows that we're supposedly engaged! That's not going to do my reputation any good, is it?'

'You should have thought of that before you said anything to your mother,' Flora retorted. Too buoyed up by the argument to feel any embarrassment about getting ready for bed with Matt in the room, she stormed into the bathroom and picked up her toothbrush.

'We had a deal,' said Matt tightly, appearing in the doorway behind her as he undid his shirt, apparently as unaware as Flora herself of how awkward the very same situation had seemed only the night before. 'We agreed that the pretence was for my mother's benefit, and that our "engagement" was to remain a secret.'

Flora squirted far too much toothpaste on her brush. 'What am I supposed to do? Tell all your girlfriends to go ahead and paw you as much as they like?' she demanded rather indistinctly as she began to brush her teeth with vigour. 'Your mother would find that very convincing!'

'Why do you have to *exaggerate* everything?' said Matt in frustration. 'There is a halfway point between acting as if you couldn't care less and clinging to me like a rash! But that would never occur to you, would it?' he added bitterly. 'You don't seem ever to have heard of the concept of balance.'

'I don't know what you're making such a fuss about,' said Flora, spitting in the basin and rinsing her teeth with bravado. 'You wanted to convince your mother that we were engaged, and that little scene today certainly did that, although she probably feels really sorry for me because you've obviously still got a thing about Venezia.'

'I have not *got a thing* about her,' he said, exasperated.

'You gave a pretty good imitation of it today!'

'I might remind you that I'm paying you a good deal of money to act out this charade,' said Matt, his mouth set in a rigid line.

'I'm not likely to forget,' said Flora, shaking her hair angrily away from her face. 'I wouldn't be sharing this room with you if you weren't paying me to do it!'

'Well, just remember it next time you feel like making me look a fool in front of other people!' he said unpleasantly, turning on his heel and stalking out of the bathroom.

He prowled around the bedroom moodily as he waited for Flora to finish. He ought to be glad that Flora had reminded him of all the reasons he found her utterly impossible. Otherwise he might have begun to find her too attractive for comfort. But now he had remembered all the things about her that drove him wild. He hated the way she made him feel that his life was running out of control. Why could she never do as she was told? And why did she always have to argue back? Life would be a lot easier if she would just be terrified of him like everyone else.

Flora didn't even look worried when she finally emerged from the bathroom. She had washed her face and her eyelashes were still wet and spiky, but her eyes were blue with defiance and her chin was set at its usual combative angle. She was wearing a blue nightshirt in some satin material. It had short sleeves and fell modestly to just above her knee, but the demure design only seemed to emphasise the inviting swell of her breasts and the legs disappearing tantalisingly beneath her nightshirt.

'It's all yours,' she said.

'What?'

'The bathroom,' Flora clarified coldly, and got into bed, determined not to show Matt that she cared in the least that he would be sleeping just inches away from her again. Last night had been difficult, but now that he had gone back to being his usual overbearing, unreasonable self it would be much easier.

That was what Flora told herself, anyway.

Matt was in a foul mood the next day, and Flora, having been woken at seven and informed that he wanted her in the office at eight to catch up on time wasted planning what he called 'this farce', was in no better temper. There was no sign of Nell, which was just as well, as they ate breakfast in frigid silence. No champagne celebrations today, Flora thought, sulkily drinking her coffee.

They got through the morning exchanging only the bare minimum of words, and the atmosphere between them jangled with unspoken tension. When a languid female voice insisted on being put through to Matt, announcing herself simply as Jinx, Flora had had enough. He could at least have made a show of not wanting to talk to any of his girlfriends while they were supposedly engaged, but no! 'Put her through,' he snapped without so much as an explanation.

Well, if his object had been to prove that he wasn't planning to let this episode change his life in the least, Flora would show him that she had no intention of changing her plans either. Picking up the phone, she called up the Travel Unit and arranged for them to organise an Australian visa for her. Since she had taken the trouble to make friends with the girls there, that was no problem, and she thought she might as well check out the cost of a round-the-world ticket while she was at it. She would have earned it by the time Nell left on Thursday!

Matt stalked out of his office when she was in the middle of comparing prices for Qantas and Air New Zealand. With a provocative lack of concern, Flora covered the receiver with her hand. 'Do you need something?' she asked coolly.

'I wanted that new sponsorship file,' he said, scowling. 'But I'll find it for myself. I'd hate to interrupt your conversation!'

'If you'll wait just a minute, I'll bring it through to

you,' Flora began, but Matt was already banging file drawers open and shut. Tight-lipped, she finished her call and then went over to push him out of the way, pull out the file and hand it to him with an insincerely sweet smile. 'Is there anything else?'

Matt practically snatched the file from her hand. 'Yes, if you've quite finished wasting company time on your personal travel arrangements, you can book a table for lunch today at that new Japanese restaurant.'

'For two?' she asked, determinedly unconcerned. She was damned if she was going to ask whom he was taking. It would be that girl with the stupid name who had rung earlier.

'Yes. One o'clock,' he said shortly, damned if he was going to explain that he was taking a contact from one of the big investment banks who had rung him earlier. He didn't have to account for all his movements to Flora. She was only his PA. 'And we'd better take Mother to the theatre or something tonight,' he added as he headed back to his office. 'Get tickets to whatever it is that everyone wants to see at the moment.'

And what was *that* exactly? Flora wondered crossly as she booked the restaurant. Who did she know who would be able to tell her what was 'in' and what was 'out'?

Seb! The answer came to her as a stroke of inspiration, and she hunted through her diary for his work number. Seb might be infuriating at times, but as a reporter he could be relied upon to keep his finger on the pulse of what was happening in the city.

Seb sounded delighted to hear from her. 'I was just thinking about you,' he said, when he had given Flora a list of shows that were both suitable for a lady in her sixties and sufficiently trendy to ensure that they were virtually impossible to get tickets for. 'I've got something to tell you. Listen, is there any chance of meeting you for lunch today?'

Flora thought of Matt eating sushi with a leggy blonde called Jinx. 'I'd love to,' she said.

'So, you've met his mother already?' said Seb, as he deposited Flora's glass on the table in front of her and slid onto the seat beside her. The pavement in front of the pub was crowded with groups of drinkers who had spilled outside to enjoy the sunshine, and Flora had had to cede half the table she had been saving to another couple. 'It must be serious between you and Matt Davenport!'

'I told you it was,' said Flora composedly. There was no reason to let Seb in on the joke yet.

'I could see that on Saturday night,' Seb admitted. 'You know, I couldn't believe that you were having an affair with a man like Matt Davenport, but there was no mistaking the way you were looking at each other at the ball.' He slid her a sideways look as he sipped his beer and grinned. 'You never looked at me like that! I'm surprised he didn't object to you having lunch with me.'

'Matt trusts me completely,' said Flora, and decided it was time to change the subject. 'What was it you wanted to tell me?'

Seb, it appeared, had applied for a post as Singapore correspondent for a sister paper in the same publishing group and thought that there was a good chance he would get it. 'I'm tired of doing "shock horror" stories,' he said. 'I want to get into more serious stuff.'

'I thought you wanted to stay in London,' Flora accused him, remembering their endless arguments on the subject.

'Only because I thought it would be better for my career. I'm prepared to go anywhere if it helps me get to the top eventually.'

That sounded like the old Seb! 'Well, good luck to you,' said Flora, raising her glass to him, and he studied her face for a moment.

'It's ironic, isn't it, that we broke up because you were so determined to chuck in everything to go backpacking around the world, and yet I'm the one who gets to travel first?' He paused. 'I suppose you'll be staying here with Matt Davenport now?'

Flora avoided his eye. 'We'll have to see how things work out,' she said guardedly. She looked over at a group of men drinking pints of beer in their shirtsleeves, and thought about Matt and how much she had wanted to run her fingers over his forearm only yesterday.

Up to this moment, she had never doubted that all she wanted to do was to travel, but Seb's question had brought her up short against the realisation that while she was travelling Matt would be in London, or back in New York, acquiring companies and driving deals and dating glamorous blondes without her. It was hard now to imagine what life would be like without him. All Flora knew was that the prospect left her feeling giddy and a little sick.

'You looked great on Saturday,' Seb was saying, moving a little closer along the bench. 'I found myself watching you and wishing that we'd never broken up. Lorna's not nearly so much fun as you, Flora.'

'Does that mean you'll be going to Singapore on your own?'

'Yes,' said Seb, looking her straight in the eye. 'But if you're ever there—with or without Matt Davenport—you'll look me up, won't you?'

Flora met his eyes directly. 'I may just do that,' she said.

After lunch, they walked back to the office together. 'I'll see you before you go, won't I?' said Flora, stopping across the road from the entrance.

'Of course.' Seb put his arms round her and gave her a hug. 'We had a good time together, didn't we?'

She looked up at him affectionately. He was right. In many ways they had grown up together. 'Yes, we did.'

'And if it doesn't work out with Matt, you'll know where to find me.'

'Yes.' With a final hug, she turned and dodged her way through the traffic to the imposing Elexx entrance, only to find herself face to face with Matt, who was approaching from the other direction.

Flora was furious to discover that her heart was bounding around her chest with pleasure at the mere sight of him, and a smile was breaking in her eyes and just curling the edges of her mouth when she remembered that he had spent the last hour with Jinx or whatever her name was. He had obviously abandoned *her* somewhere. Perhaps she had uttered some forbidden word like *feeling* or even—God forbid!—suggested that they meet again some time. That would smack too much of commitment for Matt, Flora thought sourly, managing to turn her mouth down and look suitably indifferent by the time she reached him.

'Nice lunch?' she enquired coolly.

'Very.' Never had one word sounded so much like a steel trap snapping shut. Matt had, in fact, nearly jeopardised his relationship with one of his most influential contacts by spending the entire lunch wondering whom exactly Flora was having lunch with. Their meeting had been so unsatisfactory that he had left early, apologising for his abstraction, but too restless to sit in the car. Dismissing his chauffeur, he had walked back to the office to be confronted by the sight of Flora in Seb's arms, and he had been inexplicably gripped by such a murderous rage that he could hardly speak.

'And where exactly have you been?' he managed tightly.

'Out to lunch,' said Flora.

Matt's face was set like concrete. 'Making it up with your boyfriend?' he forced himself to ask.

'Something like that.' Flora gave a careless shrug to show that she didn't mind in the least that he had seen her with Seb. 'Inviting you to the ball worked even better than I thought,' she went on with a determinedly bright smile. 'He's broken up with Lorna and is taking a job in Singapore.'

Matt had the unpleasant feeling that something hard and irresistible had struck him squarely in the solar plexus. 'I guess you'll be going to visit him,' he said through stiff lips, and Flora put her chin up. If he didn't care, neither did she!

'It'll be the first stop on that round-the-world ticket you're going to buy me,' she said.

CHAPTER EIGHT

ONLY Nell enjoyed the theatre that evening. Flora had managed to get hold of tickets to the newest musical that was getting rave reviews in all the papers, but she might as well have been watching a blank computer screen for all that she noticed on stage. She was aware only of Matt, sitting dour and set-faced beside her in the dark.

He had been in a grim mood all afternoon, and Flora herself had felt obscurely depressed. She should have been glad that she had made him realise that she was only interested in travelling, and therefore wasn't in the least likely to do anything idiotic like falling for him, but several times during the course of the afternoon she had found herself on the point of going in and telling him that she didn't really care whether Seb had broken up with Lorna or not, and that she might not go to Singapore at all.

Matt took in no more of the show than she did. The actors sang and danced interminably around the stage while he reminded himself that in three days his mother would fly to Italy and this whole farce would be over. Flora would go back to that chaotic house she shared with her friends and he would have the suite to himself again. They might even be able to get on with some work during the day. Paige would be able to join him in a few weeks, and Flora would go off to join her boyfriend in Singapore and he would forget all about her...he hoped.

Somehow they got through the evening. Nell kept the conversation going over dinner. To Matt's relief she made no comment on the strained atmosphere, although

once or twice he caught her looking at them with that
secretly amused expression that made him distinctly uneasy.

At last it was over and they could go back to the hotel.
Tonight there wasn't even anger to get them through the
awkwardness of sharing a room and a bed, and both
retreated behind a barrier of prickly politeness. Matt lay
and stared up at the ceiling and tried to remember all
those very good reasons why he didn't want to get involved with anyone, while Flora turned on her side and
made herself imagine getting off a plane in Singapore
and seeing Seb waiting for her. If she tried really hard
she could even pretend that she was looking forward to
it.

'I think I'd better get you a ring today.' Matt broke the
silence on their way to work the next morning. 'I get
the feeling Mother's not quite as convinced by our engagement as she pretends to be. Maybe a few diamonds
will do the trick.'

He had offered to meet his mother for lunch, so he
took Flora to a jeweller on the way. The limousine
dropped them in Piccadilly, at the end of Burlington
Arcade, and they walked down until they found a very
small, very discreet and very expensive shop where
nothing so vulgar as a price ticket was allowed to mar
the dazzling beauty of the gems.

Flora sat on a chair while Matt cast an experienced
eye over the tray. 'Shall we see if this one fits?' he said
in a brisk voice, picking out a spectacular sapphire and
diamond ring.

Nothing could have been less lover-like than the way
he picked up Flora's hand and slid the ring onto her
finger. It was a perfect fit. Matt grunted approvingly. 'Do
you like it?'

Did it matter whether she liked it or not? Flora looked
down at the ring and wondered what it would be like if

this were real, if Matt were buying her a ring to show her how much he loved her, to prove to the world that they belonged together, instead of to trick his mother into believing something that wasn't true.

'It's lovely,' she said a little wistfully, and glanced up to find Matt watching her with an expression that was at once unreadable and peculiarly intense. The breath dried in her throat as she gazed back at him, her own eyes blue and uncertain. They looked at each other in a timeless, wordless, unsmiling exchange that set something trembling deep inside Flora and altered indefinably the atmosphere between them, and then the jeweller was coughing discreetly and Matt was turning away to discuss the price, and she was left staring down at the unfamiliar ring on her finger and wondering what that look had meant.

'I'll give it back to you as soon as your mother goes, of course,' she made herself say when they were outside once more.

Matt strode down the arcade, his mouth set in a hard line to disguise the fact that he was feeling strangely unsettled, almost disconcerted. He had set out to shut his mother up by equipping Flora with a suitable ring, but something had happened in there. It was something to do with seeing Flora wearing the ring, something to do with the look in her blue eyes. Suddenly everything seemed *different*, and he didn't like it one little bit. He had the unpleasant sense that the smallest thing could send his feelings spinning out of control, and if there was one thing Matt hated it was feeling out of control.

'You can keep it,' he said abruptly, almost as if the words had been forced out of him.

'I can't do that,' said Flora, horrified. She was trotting along beside him to keep up. 'It's far too expensive!'

Matt doubted if she had any idea of just how expensive the ring had been, and he wasn't about to tell her. All that mattered was that he wouldn't be left with the ring as a reminder of her when she had gone. 'Look on it as a bonus for your travel fund,' he said gruffly. 'If my mother leaves on Thursday convinced that we're engaged, you'll have earned it.'

Nell was waiting for them at the restaurant, and she spotted the ring at once. 'Oh, it's *beautiful*!' she cried, taking Flora's hand so that she could admire it properly. 'You must be thrilled with it, Flora!'

'Yes,' said Flora huskily. 'Yes, I am.'

'I hope you're satisfied now,' said Matt as they sat down.

'Oh, I am,' said Nell, ignoring the irony in his voice. 'It's perfect! Aren't you glad I gave you a little prod in the right direction?'

'If you can call drawing my attention to every advertisement for diamonds, dragging me past every jeweller in London and dropping the word "ring" into your conversation at least once a minute a "little prod"!'

But Nell wasn't listening. She was twinkling across the table at Flora. 'That ring is absolutely gorgeous. You're a lucky girl, Flora.'

Flora mustered a smile. 'I know.' She was. The ring was worth more than anything she had ever owned in her life and Matt had just given it to her as a 'bonus'. She ought to be over the moon!

'I hope she's thanked you properly?' Nell was teasing Matt, and, succumbing to temptation, he brushed his thumb along Flora's jaw.

'Now you come to mention it, I don't think she has,' he said softly, and allowed himself to look deep into the warm blue eyes. They might have been alone together in the room. 'Do you really like it?' he asked her, and Flora could almost believe that it mattered to him.

'I love it,' she said. 'Thank you.' And then, because the words sounded pitifully inadequate, because it was what a real fiancée would do, because it was what she really *wanted* to do, Flora lifted her hand to his cheek, then let her fingers slide to his neck so that, when she leant into him, she could tug his head down and kiss him.

She meant just to press her lips to the side of his mouth, but once there she couldn't bear to let him go, and then Matt turned his head and their lips met with a shock of feeling that was part thrill, part recognition, a bizarre sense of familiarity, as if they had been stumbling around in the dark and had at last found their way back to where they belonged.

Matt's mouth felt so warm, so sure, so exciting, so *right* that Flora melted into his kiss, her hand creeping round to the nape of his neck to pull him closer, and when they broke for breath they could only stare at each other, shaken off balance by the piercing sweetness they had shared.

Nell was looking very satisfied. 'I think this calls for more champagne,' she said, waving over a waiter. 'Oh, by the way,' she went on when she had ordered, 'you don't mind if I don't leave on Thursday, do you? I thought I'd stay on a few more days.'

'*What?*' Matt had forgotten his mother's presence, but as her last words filtered through his attention was rudely wrenched back to her.

'I'm having such a lovely time,' his mother explained. 'And with you both spending all day in the office, I've hardly seen anything of you yet.'

'What, apart from all Sunday, all yesterday evening and this lunch?'

'You don't mind, do you, Flora?' said Nell, switching her line of attack.

Flora looked helplessly at Matt. 'What about your friends in Italy?' he asked, but his mother only waved her hand.

'They're going to be there all summer, so I can go any time. I'll just ring them and tell them I'll be a week or so later. But if you think I'll be too much trouble,' she went on with a faint suggestion of martyrdom, 'you must say, Flora.'

What *could* she say? 'Of course you won't be any trouble,' said Flora. 'It will be lovely to have you here.'

'Do you mind carrying on with this?' Matt asked in a constrained voice as they were being driven back to the office after lunch. 'If you'd rather call a halt now, I'll understand.'

'No, I don't mind going on as we are,' said Flora, twisting the ring on her finger. 'After all, I've got quite a bonus still to earn, haven't I?'

'Are you sure?' he made himself ask, and she nodded. 'I'll pay you the same rate that we agreed before,' he went on roughly after a moment, anxious to reassure her that he hadn't forgotten that theirs was a purely business relationship. Or was he the one who needed the reassurance? Matt wondered uneasily.

Flora was shaking her head. 'I don't need any more money,' she said. 'I'll do it for your mother.' Her eyes slid over to him, and then skittered quickly away. She mustered a smile, tried to sound light-hearted. 'Anyway, I've already earned enough to buy myself a first-class ticket straight to Australia. What more could I want?'

Her question hung in the silence between them. Matt looked out of the window at the traffic crawling along the other side of the Mall. 'Does that mean you're not planning to stop off in Singapore any more?'

Flora looked out of the other window at St. James's Park. 'I haven't got any real reason to stop there,' she said.

There was another long pause. She glanced sideways just as Matt turned his head, and their eyes met in a brief, charged moment as they swept past Buckingham Palace, before they both looked away again. Matt, for no readily explicable reason, felt suddenly much better.

Having spent so long over lunch with Nell, Flora spent the afternoon trying to catch up, and there was so much to do that they didn't leave the office until after eight o'clock. 'Now for a lecture from Mother about working you too hard,' said Matt wearily as he opened the door to the suite.

But Nell was just on her way out. 'You'll never guess who I met in Harvey Nichols this afternoon, Matt!' she said, kissing him on the cheek. 'The Landers!'

'That's nice,' said Matt, who had no idea who the Landers were. Obviously some friends of his mother's.

'Isn't it?' Nell agreed, pleased. 'We didn't have a chance for much of a chat, so they've invited me out to dinner. I knew you wouldn't mind. I'm sure you'd like to spend some time on your own, anyway. Oh, look at the time!' she exclaimed, bestowing a hasty kiss on Flora. 'I must go!'

'If she wanted us to have time on our own, why has she just insisted on spending another week with us?' muttered Matt, closing the door after her. 'Sometimes I could strangle my mother,' he sighed, as he came back into the sitting area where Flora was standing wondering what to do next. 'Not that it would do any good,' he added bitterly. 'I could have my hands around her throat and she'd just be saying, "I don't know why you always get so *cross*, dear"!'

He mimicked his mother with such wicked accuracy that Flora couldn't help laughing, and once she'd started she couldn't stop. Matt stared at her in surprise for a moment, before the sight of her helpless giggles broke the tension and he began to laugh too.

'It's all right for you,' he said. 'She's not your mother!'

Flora wiped her eyes. 'I think she's wonderful,' she said.

'She's not wonderful,' said Matt. 'After forcing herself on us for another week because she said she wanted to spend time with us, what's the first thing she does?

Arranges to spend the evening with people she could see any day of the week at home!'

'Perhaps she was being tactful,' said Flora, still smiling, and then she made the big mistake of meeting Matt's eyes. All at once an image of what they might be doing if they were real lovers who had been left tactfully alone for an evening seemed to shimmer in the air between them.

Matt must have felt it too, for their smiles faded slowly as the air tightened once more. They had both done such a good job of pretending to ignore the tension that had been simmering between them since that heart-shaking kiss in the restaurant. It hadn't been hostile or snappy, like before, but more of a tingling awareness of every move the other made. The laughter had shattered it, but now here it was again, gathering strength, strumming over their skin and pulsing through their veins.

'Well...' Matt forced himself to look away first. 'It looks as if it's just us this evening. Would you like to go out to dinner?'

'I'm not really hungry,' said Flora truthfully.

'Nor am I.' There was another awkward pause, and then, inevitably, they both spoke at the same time.

'I might—'

'Perhaps—'

They both stopped. 'You first,' said Matt.

'I was just going to say that I might have a shower,' she said hesitantly. 'If that's all right with you?'

'Of course.' Matt looked around him as if in search of inspiration. 'I was going to offer you a drink, and then I thought I might do some work. I've got some reports I need to read. You could watch television, if you wanted.'

Flora said that she would be happy with a book, and went off to have her shower, hoping that the quivering tension would subside if she wasn't actually looking at him. It didn't make that much difference, though. She

could picture him so clearly that he might as well have
been in the shower with her, and standing naked under
the water only made her more aware of the desire that
clogged in her throat and boomed insistently through her
body.

In the sitting room, Matt was standing by the window,
staring moodily down at Hyde Park and trying to banish
the image of Flora under the shower. He could hear the
water rushing, could practically see it beating against her
breasts and sliding down her thighs, and he turned
abruptly to pour himself another drink. He was planning
to have a shower himself when she had finished, but at
this rate his had better be a cold one.

Later, they sat on separate sofas, as far away from
each other as possible, and pretended to be absorbed in
their reading. Flora read the same page over and over
again, but her brain obstinately refused to take in a single
word. It was too preoccupied with being aware of every
single movement Matt made.

Every time he lifted his glass, every time the muscles
in his throat worked as he drank, every time he turned
a page, Flora felt desire clutch at her heart, and even
when he wasn't doing anything, when he was just sitting
there, her longing grew with every breath he took until
she was so snarled up in it she couldn't have moved if
she had tried.

She mustn't look at him, Flora told herself desperately, but her gaze kept crawling over to where Matt sat,
as if pulled by some invisible force, and she would
watch him until it was his turn to look up and their eyes
would glance off each other and then skitter away.

Matt turned a page of his report. It was about new
marketing strategies for the Pacific Rim, but all he could
see was Flora's image shimmering on the page. She
wasn't going to Singapore to be with Seb. The knowledge had been like a pulse beating insistently within him
all afternoon and now he couldn't keep his eyes off her.

She had changed into a soft skirt with a white sleeveless top and one of her shapeless cardigans that kept slipping off one shoulder. Her hair fell shining to her shoulders and her skin had a golden sheen of summer.

While she was reading, he could let his gaze linger on the line of the cheekbone, on the curve of her lips, on the fine arch of her brows, but then she would look up and he would have to drop his eyes hastily back to his report, although the words danced on the page and the only strategy that mattered was the one that would enable him to pull her into his room and spend the whole night making love to her.

The air was so charged with electricity that Flora felt as if every breath set off a chain of tiny sparks. The silence between them was intense, and she was sure that Matt would be able to hear her body beating, aching, *thundering* with desire. She would explode if she had to sit here any longer!

Unable to stand the tension, Flora got jerkily to her feet. 'I...I think I'll go to bed,' she said, appalled to hear how high and strained her voice sounded.

Matt rose instinctively to face her. 'Isn't your book any good?'

'I...can't concentrate on it,' she said breathlessly.

'I can't concentrate either,' said Matt.

'Oh?' managed Flora rather waveringly.

'Do you want to know why?'

'Why?' she whispered, as hope began to drum along her veins at the expression in his eyes, and the space around them shrank until there was just the two of them and a need that was too insistent to be ignored any longer

'Because I can't stop thinking about what it felt like to kiss you today,' said Matt, his voice so deep it sent reverberations through her. 'Because I can't stop thinking about kissing you again.'

Flora couldn't speak. She felt as if all the air had been

sucked out of her body, as if the floor beneath her feet had cracked apart and the slightest movement would send her tumbling into an abyss that was at once terrifying and tantalising and utterly irresistible.

All she could do was look back at Matt, and, reading the answering need in her face, he walked, very slowly, towards her. Slowly he reached out, and slowly he tugged the cardigan from her shoulders and down, until it fell unheeded in a soft, crumpled pile behind her.

'But *then* I think that it wouldn't be a good idea after all,' he went on softly, although his hands were drifting back up her bare arms, his fingers caressing the warmth of her skin. He could feel Flora quivering beneath his touch. 'What do you think?' he asked her wickedly.

A pulse was beating wildly in her throat, and she swallowed. 'P-probably not,' she whispered as Matt's fingers moved on to trace the line of her clavicle almost absently.

'You think it might make it awkward working together in the office?' he suggested, even as he pushed Flora's hair away from her face so that he could bend and kiss the sweet curve of her neck between throat and shoulder.

Flora gasped at the jolt of sensation that shot through her at the touch of his lips on her skin. 'It might,' she said with difficulty, as his mouth drifted devastatingly to the hollow at the base of her throat and lingered there before teasing its way up to her ear. Unable to help herself, she tipped her head back and closed her eyes with a shiver of pleasure.

'We did agree that neither of us wanted to get involved,' Matt murmured between tantalising kisses.

'Yes,' Flora agreed on a sharp intake of breath as his tongue touched her earlobe.

'You want to travel, and I want to be left to get on with running my company,' he persevered, as if he didn't know that her bones were dissolving with his nearness. 'My mother's not here, so we don't need to pretend, do we?'

'No,' she sighed, swaying closer, and she felt Matt's mouth curve in a smile against her skin.

'So you think it would be better if I stopped thinking about kissing you and tried to concentrate on my report instead?'

'It…it might be more sensible,' Flora croaked, but how could she be sensible when the briefest, feather-light touch of his mouth or his hands was enough to set her senses thrilling? She felt hollow with desire, adrift in a world where nothing mattered but the fact that Matt's lips were only inches from hers, where the ground was shifting and uncertain and the room had dissolved into a distant haze and all she wanted was for this moment to go on for ever.

Except that this wasn't enough. A deep pulse of excitement grew more insistent with every touch of his mouth, beating beneath her skin and pounding at the base of her spine.

'We should forget this, then,' said Matt in her ear.

'I know,' Flora whispered against his temple. He was so close that it was impossible not to put her hands around his neck, impossible not to turn her head and kiss his cheek, and when she had gone that far how could she not let them drift slowly along his jaw to the corner of his mouth?

'We should stop,' she breathed, and felt the crease in his cheek as he smiled again.

'The only thing is,' he said huskily, just brushing her mouth with his own, 'the thing is, Flora…I don't think I *can* stop now!'

His lips were tantalising, teasing, a torment and a delight, feathering from her mouth to her eyes, to her jaw and back to her mouth again before tracing a path of fire up to her temple. Flora sighed unsteadily and slid her hands down to spread against his shirt-front.

'I'll stop if you want, though, Flora,' he whispered. '*Is* that what you want?'

She should say yes. She should push herself away from him before she was utterly lost. Yes—that was all she had to say.

'No,' she said, putting her arms around his waist and succumbing at last to the terrible temptation to lean against him for support. 'No, I don't want you to stop.'

Matt took her face exultantly between his hands and looked down into dark, starry blue eyes, and his expression blazed with triumph and relief and something else that Flora was too giddy with longing to identify, before his mouth came down hard on hers and all conscious thought evaporated.

This was the kiss that she had been dreaming about ever since she had met him: a deep, hungry kiss that told her that his need matched hers, a kiss that fed on the excitement soaring between them and spun them out to the furthest reaches of control. Flora clung to Matt, her hands moving over him almost frantically until she found the buttons of his shirt and began to fumble them apart.

'Let's go to bed,' he murmured raggedly. He wouldn't put it past his mother to walk in with her usual impeccable timing.

Taking Flora's hand, he pulled her over to the bedroom, and closed the door firmly behind them. Leaning back against it, he yanked her ungently back into his arms for a long, long kiss before, still kissing, and unwilling to part again even for a moment, he backed her over to the bed.

Flora was shaking with anticipation, her hands so unsteady that in the end it was Matt who tugged his shirt off with one impatient movement and tossed it aside as he sat on the edge of the bed and captured her between his knees.

Drawing an uneven breath, Flora laid her hands almost fearfully on his shoulders. His bare skin was warm and sleek and hard, and she could feel the strength of him beneath her fingers. It was wonderful to be able to touch him at last, to smooth her palms along the tautly muscled shoulders and over his back, to explore the leashed power of his body.

'Flora—' Matt's back flexed in instinctive response and his voice was ragged with the effort of control. 'Flora,' he forced himself to say as he held her slightly away from him. 'Are you sure this is what you want?'

Flora leant down to kiss his ear. 'I'm sure,' she whispered, and smiled as, unable to restrain himself any longer, Matt let his hand slide luxuriously down over her hip to her calf, and then drift back up to the back of her knee and insistently over the smooth leg beneath her skirt. She kissed her way round to his other ear. 'Are *you* sure?'

His fingers tightened against her bare thigh and he looked into her face. 'I've never been so sure of anything before,' he told her.

'Good,' was all Flora said, but it was enough. Reaching down, she crossed her arms and pulled her sleeveless top over her head. Matt's face was on a level with her breasts. He gentled his hand up her spine to unclip her bra and pull it free to drop unheeded onto the floor. For a long moment, he just looked, and then, holding her by the waist, he drew her closer.

Flora gasped at the feel of his mouth against her breasts, and she twined her fingers in his hair, arching towards him, flooding with warmth. His lips and his tongue drifted from breast to breast, tasting and teasing and tormenting as wicked flames of excitement flickered over her until they exploded into one great fireball of passion. Shuddering, Flora tipped back her head and whimpered with inarticulate need.

Conscious that her growing sense of urgency matched his own, Matt fumbled at her waist until he found the fastening to her skirt and could wrench it apart. The zip was easy to undo after that, and the skirt fell in a soft puddle at her feet, leaving only her pants to slide down and discard.

And then, at last, she was naked before him, and he had time to let his hands smooth possessively up from the curve of her hips to cup her breasts before his own need grew too great to wait any longer. As he stood up to pull off his own trousers and shorts, there was a moment when they stood apart, as if on a brink, and looked at each other across the chasm, and then Matt reached out and closed the breathless gap and their bodies met unimpeded at last.

The sensation of skin meeting skin was so electrifying that Flora cried out, and Matt smiled as he drew her down onto the bed. 'This is what I wanted to do all last night,' he told her. 'And the night before that. And the night before *that*.' Rolling her beneath him, he kissed her throat, her shoulder, her breast, and ran his hand possessively over her. 'I couldn't sleep. All I could think about was touching you like this, kissing you like this, and you just lay there and slept!'

'I was the one who couldn't sleep,' said Flora breathlessly. 'I'm sure you were snoring!'

'Never!' The feel of Matt laughing swept through her with such a surge of joy that she wrapped herself around him and kissed him almost fiercely. 'Why weren't *you* sleeping?' he asked.

'I was thinking about you,' she said. 'I kept wondering what would happen if I rolled over and laid my hand against your back.'

'Did you really?'

She nodded. 'I lay there and wondered what you would do, what it would be like if you turned over as well and I could touch you like this,' she whispered as her hands roamed over him in delicious exploration. 'And like this,' she said, glorying in his hardness and his strength and the undisguised response of his body. Her fingers slid lower. 'And like this…and like this…'

'Why didn't you?' he asked with a half-groan.

'I wasn't sure you'd want me to,' Flora confessed, and Matt lifted his head to smile down into her eyes with an expression that dissolved every last doubt and sent her senses soaring and somersaulting in glorious anticipation.

'Well, now you know different,' he said. 'Or do I need to prove it to you?'

'You don't *have* to,' said Flora, pretending to consider. 'But I think it would be nice.' And then, as he secured her to him and his mouth captured hers, and just before all reasoned thought was blotted out, 'I think it would be *very* nice!'

CHAPTER NINE

LONG afterwards, when Flora opened dazed and dreamy eyes, it was with a sense of wonder that she realised that the hotel room was still there, looking exactly as it had done before. How could the world not have changed when she was so different?

She had never experienced this welling sense of fulfilment before. She felt replete, complete, almost drugged with delight. Matt had taken her with him to a different world, a different time, a different reality, where all that existed was the feel of their bodies moving together, the fire of skin upon skin and the aching tenderness of touch and taste and murmured endearments, succeeded in their turn by a wild, spiralling excitement and a pounding hunger that had driven them out to the limits of joy and then beyond into ecstasy, and left them clinging together, awed and shaken by what they had discovered in each other.

Now Matt lay with his face against her throat and his arm heavy across her. Flora moved her fingertips in delicate patterns from the dark hairs on his forearm up to the powerful biceps and smooth shoulder, savouring the sleekness of his skin. She loved the weight of him, the warmth of his breath against her neck, the feel of his chest rising and falling.

She loved everything about him.

Her hands stilled as the truth slid into her mind and lodged there, immovable, irresistible, inevitable. Flora didn't even feel surprised. It was as if she had known all along how much she loved him. How could she not have recognised what she felt for him before? Slowly, her fingers went back to smoothing over his body.

She had no future with Matt. He had made that very clear, but Flora couldn't regret what they had done. Maybe it would have been more sensible in the long run to have kept her distance and walked away with her pride intact, but what use would pride be when Paige returned and memories were all that she had left of him? She knew that she would treasure the memory of every moment they had shared that night, and right now she couldn't even feel sad to know that it couldn't last. All she felt was release in accepting how utterly she loved him, in knowing that she didn't have to pretend to herself any more. She would love Matt while she could, and when their ways parted she would go on loving him.

Instinctively, Flora knew that there was nothing she could do to change the way she felt. Yes, it might end in heartbreak, but for now all she wanted was to push the future out of her mind and make the most of the time they had left together instead. She kissed Matt's hair, and he stirred and mumbled her name into her throat with a kiss of his own, before propping himself up on one elbow so that he could look down into her face.

'That was incredible,' he said softly, smoothing a stray strand of hair away from her cheek. His eyes were alight with a warmth and tenderness that clutched at Flora's heart. '*You* were incredible.'

'Not wishing you'd got that report read instead?' she teased.

Matt's hand smoothed enticingly down to her breast, and he smiled in a way that turned all her bones to honey and sent champagne fizzing along her veins. 'What do you think?'

'You could always go and get it for a bit of bedtime reading,' Flora offered, rubbing her foot suggestively up and down his calf.

'I could, but somehow my mind's not on reading right

now!' he said against her mouth, and she wrapped her arms around his neck.

'It's probably too late to start being sensible tonight, isn't it?' she sighed happily.

'It is,' Matt agreed as she arched responsively beneath his questing hands and mouth. 'Much too late.'

When he woke long, delicious hours later, Flora was sleeping softly against him, her mouth curved in a dreamy smile. Matt hoped that she was dreaming of him. He could feel her slow, even breathing, and he was suffused with a hazy sense of contentment. Usually his mind snapped into action as soon as he opened his eyes, but at that moment all he wanted was to lie beside her and know that she was close.

Gently he reached out and rubbed a lock of her hair between his fingers, feeling its softness, before he realised what he was doing and the lazy smile was wiped from his face. Anyone watching would think that he was in love with her, the way he was carrying on!

Easing himself away without waking Flora, Matt sat on the edge of the bed and frowned unseeingly at the carpet. The last thing he wanted was to complicate his life by falling in love. Love was too messy, too demanding, too hard to control. Love was a luxury for people who had time on their hands. He had a company to run, and love had absolutely no place in his plans.

Did it?

For the first time ever, Matt was unsure of the answer. Disconcerted by his own hesitation, he pulled on a pair of trousers and bent to gather the clothes they had discarded so desperately last night. Then, still bare-chested, he sat on the edge of the bed and watched Flora as she slept.

She *wasn't* beautiful, he told himself. Her mouth was too wide, her nose too strong, her jaw too stubborn, her figure too curvy. He had known many more beautiful women, but none of them had made him feel the way

Flora did. What was it about her that made his chest tighten whenever he looked at her?

Matt looked at his watch. Nearly half-past eight. He should go to the office. He would just let Flora sleep, he decided, but he didn't want to go without saying goodbye. Ruefully he realised that he didn't want to go at all.

Placing his hands on either side of her, he bent to kiss her awake.

Flora emerged out of a wonderful dream to find that the dream was true and that Matt was kissing her, soft, tender kisses that drew her out of sleep and into a world full of sunlight. Stretching luxuriously, she smiled up at him, and he drew a sharp breath at the look in her blue, blue eyes.

'Time to wake up,' he said unevenly, and sat back before he snatched her up into his arms.

Taking the duvet with her, Flora pulled herself up, suddenly shy as the memories of the night before came flooding back. 'Have I overslept?'

'Yes,' said Matt, but when she risked a glance at him from under her lashes she saw that he was smiling, and as abruptly as it had tightened the strait-jacket of shyness dissolved and she relaxed back against the pillows.

'I'd better get up.'

'Why?' said Matt, succumbing to the temptation to reach for her hand so that he could drop a warm kiss on the inside of her wrist.

Flora felt it shiver up her arm. 'I've got this tyrannical boss,' she said. 'He makes a terrible fuss if I'm not in the office at the crack of dawn every day.'

'He sounds horrible,' murmured Matt, kissing his way up to her elbow. 'Why do you stick with him?'

'Oh, he's not so bad once you get to know him,' she managed as he reached her shoulder, and he lifted his head.

'Really?' he teased.

'Really,' said Flora, and smiled as she put her arms around his neck and kissed him. 'In fact, sometimes he's really quite nice!'

At the sight of her, warm and smiling and dishevelled and utterly desirable, something caught at Matt's heart, and he was conscious of a sudden need to tell her how she made him feel. 'Flora—' he began abruptly, then stopped. How could he explain it to her when he couldn't even explain it to himself?

Flora saw the uncertainty on his face and laid her hand on his. 'It's OK,' she said gently. 'I know what you're going to say.'

An odd expression flitted through Matt's eyes. 'You do?'

'I think so.' Flora took a deep breath. 'I think you're trying to think of a way to tell me not to read too much into what happened last night. I think you want to remind me of the agreement we made but you're afraid I'll turn emotional on you. Well, I won't,' she went on when Matt said nothing. His face was mask-like, giving nothing away. 'I'm a big girl,' she told him, making a brave attempt at a cheerful smile. 'I don't need to tell you how wonderful last night was, but it was enough for me. I don't expect anything else from you.'

'I see,' said Matt at last, in a voice devoid of all expression. He ought to be pleased that she was being so understanding. Wasn't he the one who hated scenes and clinging women who wanted him to commit and get involved?

Flora was confused by his lack of reaction. 'I mean, we know that we want different things out of life,' she said, beginning to flounder. 'Your priority is Elexx—'

'—and yours is to see the world,' Matt finished for her.

She looked down at the duvet. It wouldn't be fair on him to tell him that the only place she wanted to be now was by his side. 'Yes,' she said in a flat voice.

There was a silence. 'I'm just trying to say that last night won't change anything as far as I'm concerned,' said Flora at last, feeling that she hadn't explained herself very well.

'Do you really believe that?' asked Matt with an ironic lift of one eyebrow.

'Yes,' she said, desperate to convince herself as much as him. 'I can still be your PA until Paige comes back, and at least when we're in the office we can pretend that last night never happened.'

'And when we're not in the office?'

'Well...' Flora concentrated on pleating the duvet cover between her fingers. 'We've got to carry on pretending to be engaged until your mother leaves. It's just a few days, I know, but since we *are* going to be sharing a bed...' She trailed off and peeked a glance at Matt from under her lashes, hoping that he would help her. He must know what she was trying to say!

But Matt was just watching her with that odd, enigmatic expression. 'Yes?' he prompted.

Flora did her best to sound suitably casual. 'Well, I...um...I just thought that, since we know that neither of us expects anything, we...we might...you know, make the most of it...but not if you don't want to, of course,' she added hurriedly.

Not want to? Matt wondered if she had any idea what she did to him. She had made it clear enough that she just wanted a temporary affair, but that was OK, he told himself. He wasn't ready to commit himself to anything more than that anyway.

'Sounds good to me,' he said, and then, in case he didn't sound enthusiastic enough, he leant forward to kiss her. 'You've got yourself another deal!'

In spite of her confident assertion that they would be able to pretend that nothing had happened once they were back in the office, Flora had thought that it would in fact be difficult to work together, but there was so much to do during the day that it turned out to be not as hard as she had expected.

Matt didn't touch her in the office, nor did they refer to the long, golden hours they spent together when work was over, but sometimes their eyes would meet in spite of themselves. Neither would smile, but both would know that the other was thinking about the night to come, and Flora would go back to work zinging with happiness.

In an odd kind of way, she found it exciting, even arousing, to be coolly discussing memos and reports and communications systems with Matt when her whole body simmered with anticipation, and just looking at his fingers holding a pen or moving over the keyboard of his PC was enough to drench her with memories of how they felt on her skin.

The days spun by in a blur of meetings and pressure and deadlines to meet, while at night time stopped and there was only the enchantment, the heart-shaking delight of being together, and the glorious excitement of exploring each other's body.

Flora was in thrall, falling deeper and deeper in hopeless love each day and unable to help herself. They never spoke about the future, as if both were afraid to break the magic of the time they had together. Flora wouldn't think about what would happen when Nell left and there was no need for her to stay in the hotel any longer. She thought only about the moment at the end of every day when Matt would close the bedroom door and smile and hold out his arms.

Reluctant to share each other, they rarely went out. Once or twice Matt had to put in a token appearance at a function, and Flora went with him, but they left as soon as they could to have a quiet dinner together, or head straight back to the hotel where they spent the long, sweet hours talking, laughing and making love.

For someone who had been so keen to spend time with them, Nell was peculiarly absent during those ten magical days. She had to be the most sociable person Flora had ever met—invited out every night and breezing out of the hotel suite with barely enough time to share a drink with them when they came back from the office.

Matt and Flora were too happy to wonder where she was going, and they had almost forgotten the temporary nature of the arrangement when Nell reminded them on her way out to a drinks party that she was leaving the next day. 'Can you spare your driver to take me to the airport, Matt?' she asked. 'My flight leaves at three o'clock.'

'We'll take you out to lunch,' said Matt, 'and then I'll drive you out myself.' He hesitated. 'I'm sorry, Mother, I should have remembered myself. I'm afraid I've been neglecting you.'

Nell smiled lovingly at him. She had never seen her son so relaxed or so happy. 'You haven't neglected me at all,' she told him. 'I haven't had so much fun in a long time.'

She kissed them both and whirled out of the door to her party, leaving a constrained silence behind her as both Matt and Flora realised what her departure would mean to them.

Flora turned the sapphire and diamond ring on her finger. The stones seemed to wink mockingly back at her. 'It'll be strange not having to pretend to be engaged any more,' she said awkwardly at last.

'Yes.' Matt hunched his shoulders and prowled over to the window. Damn his mother! Why did she have to leave now? For the first time in his life Matt felt uncertain. He didn't want to have to think about what would happen next.

'We ought to agree on how we're going to end it, in case anyone asks,' Flora persevered.

'I guess so,' he said without enthusiasm. Why was *she* so keen to stick to the terms of their original agreement? She had agreed to act as his fiancée until his mother left, and that was what she had done, but that wasn't until tomorrow. She didn't have to be in quite such a hurry to finish it!

Flora eyed Matt's rigid back with increasing resentment. He wasn't exactly making this easy! They would have to decide it some time. 'We could say that you met someone else,' she suggested. 'No one would be surprised at that.'

'No!' Matt's reaction was purely instinctive. He scowled out of the window. 'Why can't we just say that we changed our minds?'

'I don't think that will be good enough,' she said, with what Matt considered heartless practicality. 'The first thing your mother or anyone else is going to ask is why.' She paused. 'Shall we say that we both got cold feet at the idea of commitment and leave it at that?' It was just about the truth, she thought sadly.

Matt didn't answer immediately. All he could think was that ending the mock engagement meant that Flora would move back to her flat and that he would be left here on his own.

He turned. 'There is an alternative,' he said, and Flora held her breath.

'What do you mean?'

'I know we agreed that we only needed to pretend to be engaged until my mother left, but we don't have to make an announcement, do we? I'd guess everyone at Elexx now knows we're supposedly engaged, and they're going to think it's strange if you carry on working for me once they've heard the relationship is over.' Matt's voice was rough with the effort of trying not to sound too eager. 'Why don't we wait until Paige comes back and you're ready to go to Australia? That would be the obvious time to break it off, anyway.'

'And in the meantime?' said Flora.

Matt walked over and put his hands on her shoulders. 'In the meantime, you'll be here if Mother happens to ring, and we don't need to explain anything to anybody. We can carry on as we are.' His fingers circled possessively, persuasively over her bare skin. 'These last two weeks have been good, haven't they?'

'You know they have,' she said. There was no point in denying it when her bones melted just to look at him, and he must be able to read the answer in her eyes.

'Then what do you say?' Matt's hands slid up to her throat so that he could caress her jaw with his thumbs. 'I don't want to tie you down, Flora,' he said as she hesitated. 'You're a free spirit; I know that. It's one of the things I l—'

He caught himself just in time. Surely he hadn't been going to say *love*, had he?

No, of course he hadn't. He never used words like love.

'It's one of the things I like most about you,' he continued smoothly. 'Neither of us is interested in any long-term commitment, but I think we've been good together, and I don't want it to end just yet. But if you want to finish it now,' he went on, 'I'll stick by what we agreed. You can take your money and we'll go back to the way we were before.'

'And if I don't want to do that?' A smile was trembling on Flora's lips and, seeing it, Matt was conscious of a giddy wash of relief.

'Stay here with me when Mother goes,' he said.

The undertone of urgency in his voice thrilled through her. 'No extra bonus?' she teased, putting her head on one side.

'No bonus,' said Matt. 'I want you to stay because *you* want to, not because of your travel fund.'

She ought to say no. The longer she stayed, the harder it was going to be to go, Flora knew that. But then, she was going to be so miserable when it ended, why shouldn't she grab at the chance of a few more weeks of happiness?

'Just until Paige comes back?' she asked, to be sure that she wouldn't allow herself any false hopes.

'Just until Paige comes back,' he said.

Flora looked up into his face and knew that she would do anything to stay with him as long as she could. She would take whatever Matt had to offer, and face the heartbreak later.

'Well?' said Matt, trying to sound casual, but she could feel the tension in his fingers, and the knowledge that he wanted her, even if only for a short time, was enough.

Smiling, she slid her arms around his waist and let the hard security of his body banish bleak thoughts of the future as she gave herself up to the simple joy of being with him for now. 'I'd like to stay,' she said.

They took Nell out for a special lunch the next day before she went off to Italy. Nell was, as always, brimming with warmth and good humour, and Flora, glowing next to Matt, reached impulsively across the table to squeeze her hand.

'We're going to miss you,' she said affectionately.

'I'll be back,' Nell promised, touched. 'And next time I want to hear some real wedding plans,' she added, with a severe glance at her son. 'No more nonsense about waiting until this deal or that deal's completed!'

'No, Mother.'

Nell rolled her eyes at his mock subservient tone. 'I don't know!' she exclaimed. 'I wonder sometimes if you know how lucky you are to have found Flora!'

Matt looked at Flora, and then at his mother. The teasing look had vanished from his eyes. 'I do,' he said quietly, and Nell nodded as if satisfied.

Reaching down, she pulled a battered leather box out

of her handbag and handed it to Flora. 'I want you to
have this,' she said.

'What is it?' said Flora, taken aback.

'Open it.'

Inside lay a delicate diamond necklace on a gold chain
burnished by many years of wear. 'Scott gave it to me
when Matt was born,' said Nell with a suddenly wobbly
smile, her throat tightening at the memory. 'But my
neck's too old to wear it now, and it feels right for you
to have it, Flora. I want you and Matt to be as happy
together as Scott and I were.'

'Oh, Nell…' Flora's eyes filled with tears. She hated
to accept anything that meant so much to Matt's mother,
but how could she refuse without hurting her more by
confessing the truth and telling her that the wedding she
looked forward to so much would never take place—or
at least not with Flora as Matt's bride?

'Thank you,' was all she said, but Nell knew that she
understood what the necklace meant.

'Don't start crying, or you'll set me off,' she told
Flora. 'And this is a happy day—you're getting rid of
me at last! I'm surprised you're not ordering champagne,
Matt,' she added with a twinkling smile.

Matt lifted a finger to attract the wine waiter's attention. 'We will have champagne,' he said, 'but not because you're going.' He waited until the champagne had
been poured and the waiter had left before lifting his
glass to Nell. 'To you, Mother,' he said, and then, while
Flora was joining in the toast, he met his mother's eyes
across the table. 'Thank you,' he added very quietly.

'It's funny, but I *do* miss her,' Flora said later that evening when they were lying together in bed, hands drifting lazily over each other. 'She was hardly ever here,
but I was really sorry to say goodbye to her.'

Matt made a non-committal noise and she poked him.
'Oh, go on, you adore her. Why can't you just say so?'

Why *couldn't* he? Matt rolled over onto his back and linked his hands behind his head. 'I guess I grew up thinking that men didn't show their feelings like that,' he said slowly. 'My mother always thought it was strange that I didn't cry more when my father died, but I thought I would be letting her down if I told her how much I missed him.'

He had never talked to her like this before. Flora settled herself into his side and rested her head on his shoulder, and Matt brought one arm down to hold her against him. 'What was he like?' she asked quietly.

Matt thought for a while. 'He was very focused, very remote except with my mother. Even as a small child I was aware of the passion between them, and, looking back, I think I felt excluded by the bond they shared. I'm not saying my father ignored me—he didn't—but I don't remember any spontaneous gestures of affection from him. All I remember is feeling that I had to do everything as well as he did.'

He paused, remembering the past, strangely comforted by Flora, warm and soft in the curve of his arm. 'My mother must have known a very different man, but to me my father always seemed inaccessible. The worst thing is that I interpreted his reserve as indifference.'

'I'm sure he must have loved you,' said Flora gently.

'He did—but I wasted twenty-nine years believing that he didn't,' said Matt with an edge of bitterness. 'It was only last year, when a good friend of his died and left me all my father's letters to him, that I realised how important I had been to him. He could tell his friend that he loved me, that he was proud of me, but he couldn't tell me himself.'

Flora heard the suppressed hurt in his voice and longed to comfort him. 'Your father was from a different generation,' she said as gently as she could. 'He probably didn't know how to express his emotions. My father's the same. He comes out in a cold sweat if anyone starts to talk about feelings. If your father had lived, he'd have been able to show you what you meant to him in other ways.'

Matt was silent, but she knew that he was listening. 'It's very sad that your father didn't feel able or didn't know how to express his love for you, but the important thing is that he *did* love you. You don't have to make the same mistake he did.'

'What do you mean?' asked Matt, stiffening in unconscious defence.

'You keep everything buttoned up inside you, just the way your father did. At least he talked to your mother. You don't open up with anyone.'

It crossed Matt's mind that he had told Flora more than he had ever told anyone before, and the realisation made him feel twitchy and uncomfortably exposed. He didn't want to 'open up' as she put it. He didn't *know* how he felt, and what was the point of telling Flora anyway, when in a few weeks she would be leaving? So, instead of explaining how much he hated the thought of her going, he tried to set her at a distance.

'I will if I ever find anyone I can trust,' he said coolly.

You can trust *me*, Flora wanted to tell him, but she sensed that he had already revealed more than he wanted to about the little boy who had grown into the man holding her in his arms. 'I hope you will,' was all she said.

It happened two days later. Matt came back from a successful meeting in the City, his mind on mergers and acquisitions, to be greeted by Flora with a list of messages. 'Oh, and can you call Tom Gorsky?' she finished, and glanced up from her notebook. 'Do you want me to get hold of him for you?'

Matt didn't answer. He was staring at her, shocked by the sudden realisation of how deeply he had fallen in love with her. '*I just looked across at her one day and knew that she was the only woman I would ever want.*'

Wasn't that what he had pretended to his mother? And now it was true.

He felt as if a fist had been driven into his stomach, leaving him winded and reeling from the force of the blow. Why now? he found himself thinking. There had been so many other times when he could have realised what Flora meant to him: when she pulled out that damned clip and shook her hair free every evening when they got back to the hotel, when she turned her head and smiled at him, when he opened his arms and she walked straight into them. But no! He had to wait until now, when her hair was primly tied up and her mind was on Tom Gorsky, to know how much he loved her.

'Are you all right?' Flora was looking at him oddly, and with an enormous effort Matt pulled himself together.

'I'm fine,' he said shortly. 'I'll talk to Tom later.' On the point of blurting out that he loved her, Matt was thrown off balance by what seemed like Flora's deliberate coolness. He had forgotten how they had agreed to remain scrupulously impersonal while they were in the office. All he knew was that he wanted to pull her into his arms and never let her go, and she was just sitting there behind her desk, being a PA.

'I've got to go down to Human Resources,' she was saying. 'I shouldn't be very long, but I may as well go now if you don't want me to do anything.'

I want you to stop being efficient, Matt wanted to shout. I want you to come over here and kiss me. I want you to tell me you'll stay here with me and forget Australia.

Flora got to her feet. 'I'll put the answering machine on,' she said, interpreting his silence as disapproval.

'I'm quite capable of answering a telephone,' snapped Matt.

Flora eyed him in some puzzlement, but decided that

JESSICA HART   161

it was safer not to comment. 'I'll be back in a few minutes,' was all she said as she went out.

Matt was still standing there looking at the door when a junior secretary from the Travel Unit knocked and came in. She looked absolutely terrified when she discovered him instead of Flora.

'What is it?' he growled.

'I've just brought Flora's passport back,' she said nervously. 'We've got her the Australian visa she asked for, and she wanted her passport back as soon as possible.'

'Oh, did she?' snarled Matt. For the first time in his life he had fallen in love, and had perversely chosen the one woman who had made it clear that her interest in him was purely temporary. Why couldn't he have fallen for one of the nice girls his mother had used to push his way, girls who wouldn't unsettle him or challenge him or spend their time running away to Australia at the first opportunity?

He took the passport and tossed it onto Flora's desk while the poor unfortunate secretary sidled out. Matt didn't even notice her go. He looked down at the passport for a long time, and then he turned with a set face and went into his room.

His door was firmly closed when Flora got back. She looked at it with a faint frown. It was usually a sign that he didn't want to be disturbed, but he hadn't actually *said* anything. He had seemed in such a strange mood when she left that it was hard to know what he wanted.

In the end, she knocked on Matt's door and put her head round it. 'I just thought I'd let you know that I'm back,' she told him. 'Were there any calls?'

'Two.' Matt was standing by the window and he turned as she came in. 'Your friend Seb called. He wants you to call him back.'

'Oh,' said Flora uncertainly. Was that the reason he was looking so grim? Surely Matt couldn't be jealous of *Seb*? 'Who else?'

'Paige.' Hunching his shoulders, Matt walked back to his desk but didn't sit down. 'Her mother is much better. Paige thinks she'll be in a position to come over and start work again in a couple of weeks.'

It was the news Flora had been dreading. She stared numbly at Matt. *'Two weeks?'*

Without thinking, Matt went over and pulled her into his arms. 'We'll make the most of it,' he promised, and Flora found herself clinging to him with a sort of desperation. She nodded, tried to smile.

'Let's go,' he said with sudden urgency.

'Go where?'

'Back to the hotel.'

Flora pulled away slightly to look up at him at that. 'Matt, it's only half-past three!'

'So?' he said, reaching for the door. 'It's my company, and I can leave early if I want to.'

He took her back to the suite and made love to her with an intensity that left them both shaken. Afterwards, Flora lay in his arms and he stroked her hair, wanting to tell her that he loved her but afraid to spoil the moment. What if she felt awkward, or embarrassed by how completely he had changed his mind? If he told her now, she might feel that he was pressurising her.

Matt knew that he was finding excuses for himself. Seb's call had shaken him more than he wanted to admit. It reminded him of all the things he wanted to forget: that Seb had known Flora a long time, that they had been lovers and friends, that the other man still felt he could call her up casually. The truth was that Matt didn't want to tell Flora because he didn't want to hear that she didn't love him in the same way, that he was still only her number two priority. The longer he kept it to himself, the longer he could hope that she too had changed her mind.

So he held her without saying anything. He would wait until they could talk things through properly, and *then* he would tell her. All he needed was the right opportunity.

Only it seemed that the opportunity was never right, and by the time the phone rang on Flora's desk a couple of days later Matt still hadn't said anything to her.

There had been times when Flora had been tempted to tell him that she loved him, but what was the point of spoiling the short time they had left together? Matt never mentioned the future. He desired her, Flora knew that, but that seemed to be as far as he was prepared to go. Once Paige came back, he would say goodbye and that would be that.

Still thinking of him, Flora picked up the phone. It was Paige, and she was obviously upset. Matt had sounded so distant on the phone, she confessed. 'I know this sounds silly, but I got the definite feeling that he didn't want me to come back and work for him again. He *said* he was glad to hear from me, but I just knew that he'd rather you stayed on, and I thought I should find out what you felt about it. If you're really happy there…'

She trailed off, but behind her calm words Flora sensed real trouble. Paige was so devoted that if she thought Matt really wanted someone else as his PA instead, she would probably offer to stand aside! If it had been anyone but Paige, Flora might even have been tempted to take on the job permanently, so that she could stay close to Matt, but her friend had had enough trouble over the last few months. It wouldn't be fair when Paige had got her the job on the understanding that she would only ever want a temporary post.

'Paige, listen,' she said, glad that Matt was occupied with a conference call to New York and couldn't hear. 'There's no question of me staying on as Matt's PA. If he sounded distant, it was probably just because he was preoccupied: things have been pretty hectic here recently. But even if he *did* offer me the job, I wouldn't accept.'

'Honestly?'

'Honestly.' Flora tried to sound cheerful and positive, like the old Flora, not the Flora who was crying inside at the thought of leaving Matt. 'I'm off travelling, remember? I'm really grateful to you for giving me this chance to earn some real money, but I've paid off all my debts and I've made my plans. I'm going to Australia, and guess what?' she went on, desperate to convince a still doubtful Paige. 'Seb's going to Singapore! I spoke to him yesterday and it looks as if we may end up travelling together after all. I'm leaving as soon as you get here, Paige, I promise. I don't want to hang around any longer.'

At least she had taken a load off Paige's mind, Flora thought, putting the phone down with a twisted smile. Sighing, she turned back to her computer, only to gasp in shock as she saw Matt. Far from being engrossed in his teleconference, he was standing in the doorway of his office and watching her with an expression that closed a cold hand around her heart.

He had heard every word.

CHAPTER TEN

PARALYSED by the sudden sight of Matt, Flora could only stare back at him for a long, airless moment.

'I just wanted to check some dates,' he said in an expressionless voice. He came over to the desk and she picked up the diary numbly to hand it to him.

'Matt—' she began, desperate suddenly to convince him that she had only been reassuring Paige, but he turned away without listening to her.

'I'm still in conference,' he interrupted her curtly, and walked into his room, shutting the door behind him.

Flora covered her face with her hands. Why had Matt had to come out just then? The look in his eyes had been so bitter that for the first time she had allowed herself to wonder if he might feel more for her than he had said, but if that was so it was imperative that he didn't think that she was desperate to go. She *had* to explain why she had sounded so dismissive about the idea of staying with him.

Jittery with nerves, Flora watched the lights on the phone for the moment Matt broke the connection. As soon as he put the receiver down, she would go in and *make* him listen, and if he realised that she didn't want to leave, and *if* she was right and he did care, perhaps—only perhaps!—everything would work out after all.

She was on her feet the moment the light for his line blinked off, but Matt came out before she even reached his door, and she could see instantly that he was not in a receptive mood. If he felt anything for her at all, he was disguising it very well. The green eyes were shuttered, his face set in hard lines.

'There you are,' he said, in a voice so cold that she flinched. 'There should be a fax coming through any second now. I'm sure you'll be interested to see it.'

'Matt, if I could just expl—' Flora pleaded, but Matt ignored her and walked over to the fax machine.

'Here it comes,' he said, as it beeped a warning and the paper oozed out. Flora watched in despair while he waited until the final beep before picking up the sheet. He glanced at it, then handed it to her, his face a mask.

'This appeared today.' His voice was biting. 'The New York office want to know if I'd like to comment.'

Baffled, Flora took the sheet. It was a copy of a page from a popular gossip magazine, and the lead item had been circled. 'FAKE ENGAGEMENT?' read the headline, and she saw in dismay that the accompanying photograph showed her with Matt and Nell. Nell was smiling, but both she and Matt looked decidedly uncomfortable. It must have been taken as they left the restaurant after Nell's farewell lunch, Flora thought irrelevantly as she began to read.

New York-based Matt Davenport, President of electronics giant Elexx, seen leaving a London restaurant with his mother, and fiancée, British PA Flora Mason (24). Although no official announcement has been made, it has been rumoured recently that Davenport is planning to marry his assistant later in the year, and Mason has been seen in his company wearing a stunning sapphire and diamond ring. But, according to a source close to the couple, their engagement is no more than an elaborate charade. Davenport (38) is apparently fed up with his mother, popular society hostess Nell Davenport, who has been urging him to get married for some years. She has dominated his life since the death of his father, Scott Davenport, whose undemonstrative nature left his son with a permanent distrust of emotional displays and a fear of long-term commitment. His mother was delighted to hear that Davenport was engaged at last, unaware that he had decided on the ruse simply to keep her quiet for a few months.

Linked until recently with British model Venezia Hobbs, Davenport came to an arrangement with Mason, who has been working for him in London. Friends of Mason said that she had been planning to travel overseas until suddenly moving in with Davenport, although she has not mentioned any plans to get married to her parents. 'We don't know anything about it,' her mother said when contacted.

'Oh, my God!' Flora put her hand to her mouth and sank onto a chair, aghast. 'They've spoken to Mum! She's going to kill me!' She lifted horrified eyes to Matt, whose face looked as if it had been carved out of granite. 'Where did they *get* all this?'

'No, that's my question,' said Matt in a glacial voice, and her jaw dropped as she realised what he was implying.

'You don't...you *can't* think that *I* had anything to do with this!'

'Well, *I* certainly haven't been confiding in Sebastian Nichols,' he said, biting off the words as if he couldn't even bear them in his mouth.

'Seb? What's he got to do with this?' Flora's appalled gaze dropped to the bottom of the article. There, sure enough, was Seb's name in bold black type. 'How could he?' she burst out furiously. 'Oh, how *could* he?'

Matt's mouth twisted into a sneer. 'What's the matter? Wasn't he supposed to tell anyone else? You can't be naïve enough to think a reporter would keep anything to himself if he thought he could make some money out of it!'

'But I didn't tell him anything. Seb didn't even know we were supposed to be engaged!'

'He's a mind-reader, then, is he?' Matt was very white about the mouth, so consumed with bitterness and hurt and anger that his only thought was to lash out. 'Is this what he wanted you to ring him about, Flora? Perhaps he wanted to check a few details with you. Hadn't he got my father's name quite right, or did he need to know whether he could say I was traumatised or just repressed?'

Flora put her hands to her ears as if to ward off the contempt in his voice. 'Matt, listen to me,' she said in desperation. 'I'm so sorry about the article, but Seb didn't get any of it from me.'

'I don't believe you,' Matt said flatly. 'You're the only one who could have known everything in that story.' His face was set in bleak, bitter lines. 'It's ironic that the first person I ever talked to about my father could hardly wait to get out of bed before rushing off to her reporter friend with all the juicy details!'

He turned away from her, unable to bear the stricken look on Flora's face. That would be a lie too, just like everything else she had told him. 'All that encouragement to open up certainly worked, didn't it? I won't be trying that again in a hurry.'

Flora felt as if she had tripped and stumbled into a nightmare. 'Look, there's been some terrible mistake—' she began, but Matt wouldn't even let her finish.

'Yes, there has,' he said in a voice so cold that he might as well have struck her. 'I made it when I trusted you.'

'Matt, *please*...'

'No!' The word was wrenched out of him, and he swore. 'How do you think my mother's going to feel when she sees this? All her friends are probably busy faxing it to her in Italy right now! But why would you care?' he remembered savagely. 'You're going travelling with Seb Nichols, who's no doubt paying for his ticket with the proceeds from that trash!'

'I'm not,' said Flora, who was beginning to feel sick with despair. It was hard to believe that this was *Matt*. Only last night he had held her in his arms and made love to her with a tenderness that had brought tears to her eyes, and now he was standing there, an implacable stranger with shuttered eyes and a harsh, pitiless mouth.

'That's not what you were telling Paige a few minutes ago!' Matt swung round to face her. 'I heard you myself—or are you going to try and deny that too?'

'No—yes—I mean, I did say that, but—'

'I don't know why I was surprised,' he interrupted her with bitter self-mockery. 'You never made any secret of what you wanted, did you, Flora? I saw you with Seb myself—I even took his messages for him—so I should have known what was going on, but all the time I let myself think that the last few weeks had meant something more to you than just the chance to earn some easy money. I guess that was my mistake too.'

Without waiting for her to answer, he strode into his room to find his chequebook. Flora, shaking, still unbelieving, followed him to the doorway. 'Matt,' she said helplessly, but he was already scrawling out the cheque and tearing it out of the book.

'Here,' he said, coming round his desk and thrusting it into her hand. 'I think you'll find that should be more than enough to cover what we agreed. I've even included a—shall we call it a gratuity?—for all those nights you worked overtime. I just hope it will mean you can stay away from London until I go back to New York!'

The colour drained from Flora's face. 'Is that it?' she said, not even looking at the cheque in her hands.

'What more do you want?'

'A chance to explain would be nice!' As if from nowhere, Flora felt anger surge along her veins, hot and blinding and gloriously invigorating. 'But you're right! What would be the point of that? You're not going to listen to any point of view but your own! It would never occur to you that you might be wrong, would it, Matt?'

Matt made to speak, but she was unstoppable now in her fury. 'If you really believe I'm capable of ringing up a reporter and tattling all your secrets, that's fine! I don't care *what* you think of me, but you know what?' she asked in a voice dripping contempt. 'The real reason I wouldn't have passed on what you said about your father is that it's not a very interesting story. It's just *pathetic* to realise that a grown man could be so incapable of expressing any kind of emotion! You blame your father, but that's just the easy way out. Other people grow up with far worse problems without turning into selfish, arrogant *bullies*!'

'I think you've said enough.' Matt's voice was like a whiplash. 'You'd better go.'

'Don't worry, I'm going!' Flora was so angry by now that she could hardly see straight, but she made it back to her desk and scrabbled through the drawers for her passport. There it was! Thank God it had come back in time!

She stuffed it in her bag and then paused to study the cheque deliberately. 'Not exactly what I'd call *easy* money,' she said, tucking it away in its turn. 'But it'll come in handy.'

At the door, Flora turned and looked back at Matt for the last time. He was standing outside his office, looking grimmer and more bitter than she had ever seen him. For a moment she was conscious of a ridiculous urge to go over and put her arms round him, but she knew that he would just push her away in disgust. He wanted her to go, and she would go.

'Goodbye, Matt,' she said, astonished at how cold and controlled she sounded. 'You know, I'm glad this has happened. I was afraid that I'd fallen in love with you, but I know now that I was just imagining things. You're so terrified of showing any emotion that you don't feel any. Nobody loves you because there's nothing about you to love,' she told him, and she turned and walked out of the door.

'Flora!' Matt strode to the door, not knowing what he wanted to say, knowing only that she was leaving. 'Flora!' he shouted after her, but she was already half-way down the corridor and she didn't even pause. She just kept on going until she had turned the corner to the lifts and then, without so much as a glance back in his direction, she had disappeared from sight.

Matt swore long and fluently. Storming back into the office, he slammed the door with a vicious kick. He wasn't going to run after her. *He* wasn't the one who had prattled about their agreement. He wasn't the one who had walked out without even an apology!

The faxed article was still sitting, discarded, on Flora's desk. Matt snatched it up, crushing it in his hand, and threw it across the room, and then, abruptly overwhelmed by despair, he slumped at his desk and dropped his head into his hands. He would have to talk to his mother and warn her about the article before she saw it, but he didn't know what he was going to do, or what he was going to say. All he knew was that less than an hour ago Flora had been humming happily in the office outside, and that now she was gone.

Flora stood by the baggage carousel at Sydney airport and watched the suitcases lumbering past. I'm in Australia, she kept telling herself, but it was impossible to accept. All those months—years!—spent dreaming about this moment, and she couldn't think of anything except how far away she was from Matt.

She fingered the ring at her throat like a talisman. Her first impulse when she had realised that she was still wearing it had been to send it back to Matt, but he had said that she could keep it. No doubt he had meant her to sell it and use the cash, but Flora couldn't bring herself to do that. It was all she had left of him, and in the end she had hung it on a chain around her neck. Now she clutched it while the memory of him twisted inside her like a knife.

Ever since Flora had walked out of Elexx that terrible afternoon eight days ago, she had been wrapped in such a fog of dull despair that she had hardly known where she was or what she was doing. It had numbed her as she threw her clothes into a bag at the hotel, isolated her from the rush-hour crowds as she sat on the bus back to the flat, and deadened her reactions the next day on the train back to Yorkshire. Flora had been grateful for its icy grip on her emotions. She hadn't even cried when her mother met her at the station in York.

The same despair had anaesthetised her on the long, uncomfortable journey out to Australia. She had done up her seat belt and got on and off planes, moving like an automaton, and none of it had seemed real. Real was Matt. Real was the smile in his eyes and the warmth of his hand and the glow that came from just being near him. Flora felt cut off from the world without him, as if she had lost the part of herself that could think and feel and respond.

She ached for Matt with a sharp, persistent ache that reverberated along her bones and nagged at her nerves and throbbed even at her fingertips. Flora felt as if the ache was the only part of her that really existed, and she was afraid that if it went away it would leave her hollow and meaningless.

She had to put Matt behind her; she knew that. He hadn't tried to contact her once since she had left. He knew where the flat was, so he could have found her if he had wanted to that first night before she had fled up to Yorkshire. He could have rung, but he hadn't, and that meant that he didn't want to find her. And if he really believed that she had had anything to do with that article, Flora didn't want to be found.

That was what she had told herself when there was no sign of Matt at Heathrow. She had known that he wouldn't be there, but it hadn't stopped her hoping against hope that he would miraculously appear and snatch her into his arms and refuse to let her get on the plane. And now she was here in Australia, with no option but to start afresh. She was going to put Matt behind her and discover a new life for herself, and pretend that that was what she had wanted all along.

Well, she would try.

Flora's bag trundled into view at last, and she hoisted it off the carousel and onto her trolley. She had no idea where she was going to go, or what she was going to do next, and suddenly she was overpowered by such a terrible feeling of hopelessness that all she could do was cling onto the trolley in panic. She didn't want to be here! She wanted to be back in London, lying in bed next to Matt, running her hands over his sleek, strong body, savouring the taste of him and the feel of him and the sound of him breathing.

Aware of a few curious glances being cast in her direction, Flora made an immense effort. She couldn't stay here for ever. Squaring her shoulders, she headed towards the customs area. She had nothing to declare but a broken heart, and Flora didn't think the customs officer would be particularly interested in that.

And then it was out through the doors and into the terminal, which was thronged with people waiting to greet relatives and friends arriving from London. Amidst the hubbub, Flora could hear the squeals of excitement as a loved one was spotted and swept into a joyful welcome. Keeping her eyes down, Flora pushed her trolley past them. There would be no one to meet her.

Pain squeezed her heart with cruel fingers, but she forced down the tears. She had spent the last few days with her parents stony-eyed, too sick with misery to cry, and she wasn't going to start crying as soon as she arrived in Australia. She *wasn't*.

'Flora?'

Flora heard her name, but the American voice was so like Matt's that she recognised it as a ghastly trick of the mind. It was wishful thinking to imagine that Matt could be here, waiting for her, she told herself bitterly. Did she really think that wanting something enough would make it happen? Closing her eyes briefly in anguish, she tightened her grip on her trolley and pushed desperately on.

'Flora!' There was someone beside her, a hand touching her arm.

Flora froze. It *sounded* like Matt, but it couldn't be him...could it? She turned her head very slowly, fearfully, bracing herself for the blow of discovering that it wasn't him at all, and her heart stopped. There he stood, tall and dark and powerful. The same uncannily light green eyes, the same fierce brows, the same cool, severe mouth that had turned her bones to honey. No one else had a mouth like that.

It was Matt. It *was* him!

She stared, incredulous, still not daring to let herself really believe that he was there, standing before her, his expression taut and uncertain as if he, too, couldn't accept that he had found her.

'Matt?' Flora's voice was barely more than a thread, and her knuckles stood out white where she gripped the trolley for support in a world that suddenly staggered around her.

Matt nodded. He couldn't speak. All he could do was drink in the sight of her. She looked thinner, somehow muted, and the blue eyes were dark with despair, but it was Flora, at last.

'I was afraid I'd missed you,' he said suddenly. His voice was hoarse, and once he had started, the words came tumbling out in an unstoppable rush. 'I've been waiting and waiting for you to come through that door. I was beginning to think that I hadn't seen you, that you'd slipped past in the crowd, that you'd gone and I'd never be able to find you again.'

Flora felt curiously disjointed. She heard his words but they didn't make any sense. Nothing made any sense any more. She moistened her lips. 'Wh-what are you doing here?'

'I had to see you,' said Matt, oblivious to the fact that they were standing right in the middle of the exit and that other passengers were having to manoeuvre their trolleys past them with difficulty. 'I had to explain, to apologise—' He broke off and closed his eyes in defeat. 'God, I just had to see you,' he admitted. 'I've missed you so much, Flora. I had to see you and tell you how much I loved you.'

And then, because he'd said what he had come to say, he stopped and waited, his green eyes shadowed with anxiety.

'Oh, Matt...' Flora whispered as his words sank slowly into her heart, and she let herself believe that wanting something enough could make it happen after all. The tears that she had held so resolutely at bay shimmered in her eyes as she stared at him. He loved her! He had said that he loved her!

'Oh, *Matt*...' It was all she could say. She let go of the trolley and took an unsteady step towards him, moving jerkily like a puppet as shock, hope and the dread that this was just some wonderful dream which would evaporate at any moment struggled within her. 'Oh, Matt!' she said again, reaching for him blindly, and then his arms were around her, holding her so tightly that she could hardly breathe, and she was clinging to him as if he might vanish at any second.

Her face was buried in his shoulder and Matt rained a frenzy of kisses on her hair. 'I love you, I love you, I love you,' he told her in a ragged voice. 'I can't believe I'm holding you again at last. It's all I've thought about since you walked out that day. I've come halfway round the world to find you, Flora,' he said. 'Say you love me too.'

'I do, I do,' Flora wept, kissing his throat, his jaw, any bit of him she could reach. 'Oh, Matt, I've been so miserable! All I wanted was to see you again, and now you're here and I can't believe it; I can't take it in. I know this is the happiest moment of my life but I can't stop crying.'

Matt turned her head between his hands so that he could look down into her tear-streaked face. The blue eyes were starry between wet, spiky lashes. Very gently, he wiped the tears from her cheeks with his thumbs. 'Say it again,' he demanded urgently. 'Tell me you love me.'

'I love you,' she said, and at last Matt let himself believe that it was going to be all right. His eyes lit with an exultant smile and he caught her back to him, and they kissed, a deep, frantic kiss that said more than words ever could about the loneliness and despair and desperation they had known when they were apart.

'Flora, darling, I'm so sorry for all those things I said to you,' he said when he could speak, holding her a little away from him and taking her hands in a tight clasp.

'It doesn't matter,' Flora began, but he shook his head.

'It *does* matter. I should have trusted you. I *knew* what you were like, that you would never have said anything to anyone about our agreement, let alone about my father. It was just that, when I rang New York and they read out what Seb had said, I was so angry I couldn't think straight.'

His fingers tightened around Flora's, willing her to understand. 'I'd never told anyone how I felt about my father. You were the only person I'd ever felt close enough to talk to, and it seemed as if I'd finally learnt to open up, only to be slapped in the face. And I was

already sick with jealousy,' Matt went on with a rueful
smile. 'I'd just spent days plucking up the courage to
tell you that I loved you, and there you were telling
Paige that you were planning to travel with Seb after all.
The next thing, I was presented with an article that he'd
written about us...and then everything seemed to fall
horribly into place.'

'Matt,' said Flora lovingly. 'How could you possibly
think I'd rather be with Seb than with you after those
weeks we'd spent together? Couldn't you tell how much
I loved you whenever you kissed me?'

'I wasn't sure,' he admitted, pulling her back into his
arms and resting his cheek against her hair. 'I wanted to
tell you how I felt but I didn't dare. Do you remember
what you said when you left? That there was nothing to
love about me?' He shushed Flora's protest. 'I know you
didn't mean it, but I think that deep down that's what
I'd felt about myself since my father died. Because I
thought he hadn't loved me, I didn't think anyone
could.'

'Matt, I'm so sorry,' murmured Flora. 'I was just saying what I thought would hurt you, because you'd hurt
me.'

'I know,' said Matt, kissing the soft, silky hair. 'In
any case, it didn't take me long to realise that you were
wrong about one thing. I sure did have feelings, and they
were all about you!'

Flora tilted her head back to look up at him. 'When
you heard me telling Paige about travelling with Seb, I
wasn't telling the truth. I was just trying to reassure her
that I wasn't planning to do her out of a job.'

'Yes, she told me,' said Matt, to her surprise.

'She *told* you? You mean you've talked to Paige about
us?'

'Now I've learnt to express my emotions, there's no
stopping me!' he teased. 'Besides, I was desperate to
find you and I thought she might be able to help me.'

Belatedly noticing the crowds manoeuvring past them, he took hold of Flora's trolley but kept one arm securely around her. 'Let's get out of here,' he said. 'I'll tell you the rest on the way to the hotel.

'It took one night without you to realise how much I needed you,' he went on once they were ensconced in the back of a sleek limousine that bore them noiselessly towards the city centre. 'I didn't care about the article, or what you had or hadn't said to Seb. I just needed to be with you.'

He lifted Flora's hand and kissed her palm before twining his fingers tightly with hers. 'My first thought was to go round to your house as soon as I could the next day, but there was no one there. I had a feeling you would have left London as soon as you could, and I guessed that you would go to your parents, but all you'd told me was that they lived in Yorkshire, which wasn't much to go on. I checked your personnel records but they only gave your London address, so they weren't much help, and then I remembered that Paige was a friend of yours. I was too desperate to think about the time difference. I must have woken her in the middle of the night to tell her everything and beg her to help me find you.'

Flora began to laugh, picturing Paige's reaction at discovering that her cold, calculating employer had feelings after all. 'Was she very shocked?'

'I guess she was a bit surprised.' Matt smiled. 'But it takes a lot to throw Paige. She said she'd been to visit your parents once with you, but all she could remember was that you'd taken the train to York. That was more specific than Yorkshire, but not much! I was all set to drive up and look round for a village with that medieval church you described on a hill when Mother rang.'

'Nell!' Flora clapped her free hand to her mouth. She had completely forgotten about Matt's mother. 'Poor Nell! Was she terribly upset by Seb's article?'

'Not nearly as upset as she was to find out that I'd lost you!' Matt said with wry amusement, remembering his conversation with Nell. 'She hasn't spoken to me like that since I was a small boy, and I felt about five by the time she'd finished with me! I'll spare you the colourful language, but I gathered I was a stubborn, selfish fool who'd made a complete mess of the best thing that had ever happened to me. Then, having reduced me to a gibbering wreck, she admitted that it was all her fault!'

'*Her* fault?'

'Apparently she met Seb at some reception she got herself invited to. He introduced himself to her and said that he knew you, but forgot to mention that he was a reporter. Mother's always had a soft spot for charming young men, and it sounds as if Seb set out to be very charming indeed. She's so indiscreet that it didn't take him any time to find out her life history, right down to her worries about the effect my father's death had had on me.'

Flora turned in her seat to look at Matt with a puzzled expression. 'But Nell couldn't have told Seb that we were just pretending to be engaged! She didn't know that.'

'Didn't she?' Matt's smile was ironic. 'I always forget how easy it is to underestimate my mother,' he said with some feeling. 'She knew long before I did that I was in love with you, but she could see that things weren't right between us. She guessed right away that we weren't really engaged.'

Flora thought back to the disconcertingly shrewd look in Nell's eyes sometimes. 'I wondered sometimes...but it doesn't make sense! Why didn't she say anything if she thought we were lying?'

'Because, Mother being Mother, she thought all we needed was a little push in the right direction. She liked you at once, so she played along with the engagement idea, and even stayed on an extra week to make sure that we couldn't just drop the pretence as soon as she left. That's why, having insisted that she wanted to get to know you better, she went out every night. She wanted us to spend all our time together, and it worked, didn't it?'

They looked at each other and smiled, remembering the long, sweet summer evenings spent making love, falling in love. 'Yes,' said Flora softly, 'it did.' And Matt kissed her again.

Later, she stood on the balcony of the hotel room and looked out at Sydney Harbour spread out before her. There was the Opera House, with its extraordinary roofs; there was the famous bridge. Little boats bobbed at their moorings, and in the distance a whole company of yachts unfurled their sails as they raced out towards the ocean, skimming through the glittering water.

Flora drew a jubilant breath. She had had a shower and it felt as if the last, lingering traces of despair had been washed away with the grime of the long journey, leaving her refreshed and energised and every sense fizzing. The sky was a bright, exhilarating blue and the very air seemed to sparkle and shimmer with vitality...but maybe that was just the joy dancing along every fibre of her being. Matt's arms enclosed her and she leant back against his chest, smiling as he kissed her neck in a way that sent a shudder of happiness down her back to clench at the base of her spine.

'You still haven't told me how you found me.'

Matt rested his chin on the top of her head. 'Where had I got to? Oh, yes, Mother's call...well, she'd cleared up how Seb seemed to know so much about us, but I was still no nearer to finding you. So I called the one person who could help me: Seb.'

'*You* rang *Seb*?' Flora twisted in his arms and stared up at him in disbelief.

'He said in the article that he'd spoken to your mother, so I knew that he had their number at least, and, since you'd been friends some time, the chances were that he'd know where they lived anyway.'

'But how could you bear to speak to him after what he'd written about you?'

Matt shrugged. It was hard to believe how angry he had been now that he had Flora safely back in his arms. 'I didn't care what I had to do as long as I could find you,' he told her. 'Seb more or less confirmed what Mother had told me. He'd been pretty much convinced by seeing us at the ball, but Mother's hints that we weren't quite what we seemed made him think again, and it wasn't that difficult for him to fill in the gaps by guesswork.'

'It was none of his business,' said Flora, trying to sound cross, but, like Matt, unable to care very much now that they were together again.

'I gather it was too tempting a bit of gossip for him to resist, but if it's any consolation he did apologise for the trouble it had caused. He said he'd offered the story to a US magazine in the hope that you would never see it, but he didn't take the efficiency of Elexx's Media Relations Unit into consideration.

'Anyway,' Matt went on, seeing that Flora remained unconvinced, 'I promised him as many in-depth interviews as he wanted if he'd just tell me where your parents lived, but I still had to work out what I was going to say to you. I didn't want to talk to you on the phone— I'd treated you too badly for that—so I thought the best thing would be to go up and see you. I drove up to Yorkshire the next day, but when I got to the house there was no one there. I sat outside for what seemed like hours until your parents came back from putting you on the train in York. You can imagine how I felt, knowing that I'd missed you by a matter of minutes!'

'If only I'd known you were coming,' said Flora, putting her arms around his waist and resting her head against his shoulder. 'I was so unhappy, I didn't know what to do with myself. It was my father who said that I should go straight to Australia, as I'd planned, and he got me a seat on the first available flight. I spent that night in London and flew out the next evening.'

'I know. Once I'd explained everything to your parents, they told me what flight you were on. I was going to drive straight back down to London and see you before you left, but I couldn't help remembering everything you'd said about wanting to see the world, and I thought if I could just get here before you we could have a fresh start, away from everything. Your father drove me to Newcastle and I got the shuttle down to Heathrow just in time to catch the Sydney flight that night.'

Matt smiled ruefully at the memory. 'I always have my passport with me, so that wasn't a problem, but I had to buy a change of clothes when we stopped in Bangkok. I got here yesterday morning, and all I could do was wait for you. It was the longest twenty-four hours of my life, Flora,' he said, twining her hair in his fingers so that he could tip back her head. 'I can't tell you how I felt as I stood there and waited and waited for you to come through that door, and then suddenly...there you were.'

'And now here we are,' said Flora, smiling up at him with such love in her eyes that Matt caught his breath.

'Here we are,' he said slowly, and wondered if she would ever know how much he loved her.

'Just the two of us.' Flora was teasing a suggestive trail of kisses along his jaw. 'Quite alone...with nothing to do.'

Matt smiled as her lips brushed his mouth. 'Well, there is *one* thing we could do,' he murmured as she kissed her way along the other side.

'So there is,' she whispered provocatively in his ear. 'We could ring your mother and tell her she can look forward to being a grandmother after all.'

'We could,' Matt agreed, and took her hand to pull

her unresisting back into the room where the wide bed waited invitingly. 'But let's do it later!'

Much, much later, Flora stirred and stretched contentedly beneath Matt's possessively drifting hands. 'So all those stories we made up for Nell were a complete waste of time?'

'Oh, I don't know,' said Matt, pretending to consider the matter. 'We don't need to plan the wedding, because we already know that we're going to walk from the church and that there'll be a marquee in your parents' garden decorated with that—what was that flower called again?'

'Cow-parsley.'

'Right...decorated with cow-parsley,' he finished, and Flora laughed.

'And you don't need to buy me a ring either,' she reminded him, reaching for the chain that had been discarded earlier on the bedside table. She dangled it from her fingers and the diamonds flashed in the sun.

'True.' Smiling, Matt unfastened the chain and let the ring drop into his hand. He held it for a moment and then, propping himself above Flora, he took her hand and slid the ring back where it belonged. 'I love you,' he said, looking deep into her eyes, and she put her arms around his neck.

'I love you, too,' she said softly, and drew him down for a long, long, dizzyingly sweet kiss.

'*And* we don't have to waste time discussing the honeymoon,' Matt remembered some time later. 'What was it you told Mother we were going to do?'

She kissed his shoulder. 'We were going to sit on sand dunes and watch the sunset...and lie on white beaches and listen to the coconuts drop!'

'That's right,' he said, his fingers smoothing lovingly over Flora's bare stomach. 'And then there were all those long, hot tropical nights...'

'I seem to remember I also said something about divorcing you if you even thought about contacting the office,' Flora pretended to warn him, even as she quivered beneath his touch.

Feeling her response, Matt smiled. 'You don't think you'd be open to negotiation on that one? I might have to make one or two calls, but otherwise I figure they can manage without me for a while. I can't manage without you,' he told her, shifting so that he could begin pressing kisses along her shoulder to the base of her throat.

'I'm sure we could come to some agreement,' said Flora contentedly. 'We're good at agreements, after all!'

She felt the laughter shake Matt's frame. 'So we are,' he said. 'It seems that you were right all along.'

'I *was*?'

'You said we were made for each other the first day we met,' Matt reminded her. 'And we are, my darling, we are!'

In 1999 in Harlequin Romance® marriage is top of the agenda!

Get ready for a great new series by some of our most popular authors, bringing romance to the workplace! This series features gorgeous heroes and lively heroines who discover that mixing business with pleasure can lead to anything...even matrimony!

Books in this series are:

January 1999
Agenda: Attraction! by Jessica Steele

February 1999
Boardroom Proposal by Margaret Way

March 1999
Temporary Engagement by Jessica Hart

April 1999
Beauty and the Boss by Lucy Gordon

May 1999
The Boss and the Baby by Leigh Michaels

From boardroom...to bride and groom!

Available wherever Harlequin books are sold.

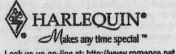

HARLEQUIN®
Makes any time special ™

Look for a new and exciting series from Harlequin!

HARLEQUIN Duets™

Two __new__ full-length novels in one book, from some of your favorite authors!

Starting in May, each month we'll be bringing you two new books, each book containing two brand-new stories about the lighter side of love! Double the pleasure, double the romance, for less than the cost of two regular romance titles!

Look for these two new Harlequin Duets™ titles in May 1999:

Book 1:
WITH A STETSON AND A SMILE
by Vicki Lewis Thompson
THE BRIDESMAID'S BET
by Christie Ridgway

Book 2:
KIDNAPPED? by Jacqueline Diamond
I GOT YOU, BABE by Bonnie Tucker

2 GREAT STORIES BY 2 GREAT AUTHORS FOR 1 LOW PRICE!

Don't miss it! Available May 1999 at your favorite retail outlet.

HARLEQUIN®
Makes any time special.™

Look us up on-line at: http://www.romance.net

HDGENR

✦ Harlequin Romance®

Coming Next Month

#3547 DADDY AND DAUGHTERS Barbara McMahon
Jared Hunter had just discovered he had not one but *two* adorable two-year-old daughters he'd known nothing about! Cassie Bowles was more than willing to help this bachelor dad with his newfound family. But could she accept his marriage proposal, knowing he only wanted a mother for his daughters?

Daddy Boom: *Who says bachelors and babies don't mix?*

#3548 BEAUTY AND THE BOSS Lucy Gordon
Parted temporarily from those he relied on—his young daughter, Alison, and his beloved guide dog—Craig Locksley was forced to accept Delia's offer of help. So Delia found herself living with an impossibly grumpy but incredibly attractive man. She wanted to love him—if only he'd let her....

Marrying the Boss: *From boardroom...to bride and groom!*

Introducing the second part of Rebecca Winters's wonderful new trilogy:

#3549 UNDERCOVER BACHELOR Rebecca Winters
Gerard Roch had given up on love since the death of his first wife. Going undercover to catch a thief, he never expected to find himself attracted to an eighteen-year-old temptress. But was Whitney Lawrence really what she seemed...?

Love Undercover: *Their mission was marriage!*

#3550 HER OWN PRINCE CHARMING Eva Rutland
Brad Vandercamp is a millionaire English playboy so glamorous that his nickname is Prince! And when Paula meets him at a glittering masked ball, she realizes that she could have found her very own Prince Charming. But they are worlds apart—she's poor, he's rich. Could he really want her for his bride?